Big Noise at the Funky Butt Jass Club

by Eric Moberg

ISBN: 978-1480044593

Cover art by Kevin Rampone

This is a work of fiction. With exception of historical personages, any other resemblance to real persons is coincidental.

Prologue

Yep, Honey Boy Golden was the one who started it all.

> Woke up this mornin'
>
> Heard my mother say
>
> 'Take your funky little butt,
>
> Go outside and play'

Right about 1900, down in New Orléans it was.

New Orléans was a creation of the River—the great River, the River that divides the country as it joins it, almost too wide to see the other shore at places but only ankle deep in much of it. New Orléans is a city on the Gulf and a city that became, by simple geographic destiny, a center of commerce between the heart of America, the plantations of the Caribbean, the markets of Europe, and the slave-trade with Africa. Some scoffed, some cried, some laughed, but many rejoiced when Jefferson negotiated the Louisiana Purchase for $5 million in 1803. To many, that was a fair price for the city of New Orléans alone, the city on the River, the birth place of Jazz.

Many may have taken this or that credit, like Jelly Roll Morton, but he didn't really invent jazz music. He may have been the first to write it down and sell it to publishing companies, but he was still in diapers when the wondrous boy brought blues, rag, and gospel together in one, sprinkled some military march attitude on it and set it all to African drum beats—Jass. That's what they called it once they started calling it anything; for a long time, it was just "dance music." The dancers called it "hot" when it was up-tempo or "sweet" when it was slow and sultry. Some of the piano players continued to call it ragtime until the day they died. Eventually, America—and the world—would call it "jazz." It would later branch off into swing, rhythm and blues, rock and roll, disco, funk, soul, grunge, and even hip hop.

But if you listen closely to anything that came after jass, you can hear Honey Boy Golden—the one who started it all.

Wondrous Honey Boy

"Mr. Honey Boy don't play trumpet."

"No?"

"No ma'am."

"What does he play, then, cornet?"

"Neither, Mr. Honey Boy plays Honey Boy," explained Bessie as the two approached the club.

"Yes, yes" added Zora growing more excited as they grew nearer, "he plays everything: waltzes, polkas, mazurkas, blues…"

"Honey Boy plays jass, hot jass—Honey Boy style. He drops a big four; he drawls."

"Yes, yes; he lilts, like a summer afternoon in Louisiana."

"And tonight, just before midnight," Bessie paused for effect just before the two entered the club, "he wants to hit a 'double G.'"

"A 'double G'? How can he do that?" asked Zora, "That's above 'double C,' and who can even hit that, except maybe Freddie Rampart or King Louis?"

Where was Honey Boy?

Professor Tony walked up toward the piano between songs, so Little David stepped aside as not to insult the instrument. David often sat in with bands at the hall while on break from his brothel gig around the corner. The Professor often joined Honey Boy's trio plus Red on guitar. This was a formidable quartet, mixing youth with experience, classical training with god-given passion.

Deacon Jones dug cemetery plots during the week but tended bar on weekends and holidays to earn extra money to send his son off to seminary. Jonesy mixed his mysterious concoctions at the bar while Hoodoo Sister Ethel nursed her champagne and reminisced. "Come on in here," Ethel whispered to Sergeant Hill.

Jonesy mixed his mysterious concoctions at the bar while Hoodoo Sister Ethel nursed her champagne and reminisced. She had a calming influence on all in her presence. Her eyes seemed always to engage whomever she encountered, and her face beamed with compassion, which endeared her to all as if she were everyone's favorite aunt.

"Come on in here," Ethel whispered to Sergeant Hill.

Sergeant Hill of the New Orléans Police pretended not to hear as he peered in from the dark kitchen where he lurked in his baker's apron disguise, most assumed in surveillance of the establishment in preparation for the raid that all the regulars knew was overdue. But the sergeant was actually trailing his unrequited lover, who was presently dancing with another man.

A blonde Russian artist named Karnofsky stood in the well-lighted corner sketching portraits later to render in paint from her late night studies. This was more than a dance or a hall or an event. It was a way, a new way—the New Orléans way.

This was Honey Boy's domain.

The adult playground city of New Orléans derived its name from a younger brother of Louis XIV: Philippe I, *Duc d'Orléans* and his son, Philippe II. The elder had a reputation for being an unabashed homosexual and the younger, a reputation as an unrepentant hedonist. The cruel rumored explanation for Philippe I begetting a son was that he had managed to find a woman to marry who was ugly enough to look like a man. As nephew to the king, Philippe II became Regent of France for over a decade while the great grandson of dearly departed Louis XIV grew to majority. The young *Duc d'Orléans* made much of the post, moving the Court from Versailles back to Paris, reinventing French cuisine, and hosting a seemingly endless party of unparalleled debauchery. He was not without his qualities, though, Philippe was an accomplished chemist, mathematician, and musician.

Bessie and Zora were music tutors at the Fisk School in New Orléans. Bessie was voluptuous and worldly; her hair and skin were deep black. She walked with the confidence and purpose of a victorious general. Zora, whose older brother described as a "bean-pole," was athletically slender and tall—taller than the average man. Her skin and hair were a deep, earthy brown. Her countenance and posture were proud and proper. Bessie and Zora each had her own style and charm. The two worked as bar girls in Storyville just as Storyville worked them, each exploiting and complementing the other. They were the pretty and innocent girls who drew the men in, enticed them to buy over-priced drinks, and led the inebriated to empty the remainder of their wallets with the rougher gals who worked "back stage." The infamous hottest district of New Orléans hosted the busiest sporting houses in Ol' Dixie.

But Where was Honey Boy?

Zora looked around at it all, "I can't believe this place is in the middle of all these—"

"Where else would they put it?" Bessie interrupted.

The Funky Butt Jass Club was a happening more than a place. It was an experiment and celebration of freedom of former slaves and their children. Sunday night was slow at the sporting houses, so half the working women and bar girls took a break from entertaining their patrons and sought their own refuge, others sought their own pleasure. Bessie and Zora became regulars at the Jass Club, for the music, and the refuge, and the pleasure.

"If you take off the 'J,' you have 'ass'," Bessie observed as she gazed at the faint sign on the wall of what, by day, was officially know as the Sons of the Union Hall. After paying their hard-earned nickel entrance fees, the girls breathed in the heat, the sweat, the smoke, the whiskey, the lust, and the beat—the big-four beat—Honey Boy's big-four beat—the beat that dropped every-other time—the syncopated rhythm that sounded like freedom—freedom from Africa, freedom from Europe, freedom from the Delta, freedom from Jim Crow. Honey Boy and his big-four beat mocked the Jim Crow minstrelsy that failed to mock Honey Boy. Honey Boy was too big; he was too loud; he was too bold; he was too brilliant. Honey Boy shone. The later the night got, the brighter he shone, like a black star in the blue night.

"Mr. Honey Boy doesn't play minstrels," Zora commented, mostly to herself.

Bessie added, "All dance music."

True, he played all types of dance music, until midnight. After midnight, though, the Funky Butt Jass Club became more than another dance hall, it became Honey Boy's domain. Honey Boy held court; he was royalty. Before King Oliver, before Duke Ellington, before Count Basie, before Lady Day there was Honey Boy Golden; he was the father of it all, and before he walked away from it all, he had it all, and then some.

The band was hot, the band was sweet. The floor was wood, Southern Yellow Pine from up the river, somewhere. It swelled with the humid weather and rocked with the dancers. The dancers were part of the band. The musicians played to the dancers as the dancers played to the musicians.

"My shoes are about to dance right off my feet," Bessie announced.

The shoes stomping and shuffling on the floor raised the dust as the stomps echoed beneath and above the hollow crawl space of the foundation below, turning the hall into a giant drum played by the crowd's feet to the beat of the band. The crowd knew Honey Boy's beat—the beat that inspired as it hypnotized, energized and mesmerized. His was a beat that could call his children home and away from Lincoln Park, over to Johnson Park where Honey Boy would play, drawing the crowds from rival bands at the edge of Storyville.

Storyville was zoned for semi-sanctioned prostitution and named for Alderman Sidney Story, who codified the district, hated jazz, but loved Strauss and his waltzes. Rather than actually permitting vice in Storyville, Alderman Story's Ordinance No. 13,032 simply outlawed it everywhere else but Storyville. The Alderman chaffed at the press coining the appellation "Storyville" for what the locals simply called "the District." The legal experiment commenced on New Year's Day of 1898, and only began to disestablish in 1917 when Secretary of War Newton D. Baker banned prostitution within five miles of any installation of the United States Army. After New Orléans Mayor Behrman visited Washington to lobby for a reprieve, Daniels offered only this ultimatum: "Either you close the red-light district… or the

United States Army will." Daniels was a moral and ethical man who did not pander, swear, or even drink.

When would Honey Boy show?

Bessie and Zora were accustomed to the burning sweet taste of whiskey; it was a taste that had grown on Bessie since she was twelve and on Zora since last month, but not so much. Drinking whiskey was a clear sign to the men at the club that these women were available. The girls hardly needed to advertise, though, with their black and gold striped Paris leggings, red satin New York dresses, and white linen St. Louis petticoats, all gifts from Little David, the piano player want-to-be pimp who courted them.

"Let's be sure we got partners before too late," Bessie advised Zora.

Zora nodded knowingly, "sure, sure."

Indeed, the young women didn't want to be unaccompanied when midnight struck and Honey Boy played the blues, the deepest blues, the sweetest blues, the blues that enchanted—a blues that syncopated equal parts soulful emancipation and carnal lust. If you didn't have a dance partner by midnight, you may as well take a seat to watch or just go home. Once a couple joined, there was nothing between them but desire and no time for second thoughts or second chances. Before midnight the dancing was big and joyous and proud, the floor was packed as it pulsed and pounded. After midnight the crowd thinned and the dancers tightened into themselves, into their couple, into their passions, into their desires.

Honey Boy's horn was just as loud, just as proud after midnight as before midnight, but his notes hung in the smoky air and in the lusty ears for ever so slightly longer, long enough for the dancers to contemplate love and life. Honey Boy's blues had what musicians would later call "swing." Technically, The Golden band played what composers would describe as a triplet—three notes played in the space of two notes. Somehow the triplet created a space, a space between.

What was Honey Boy doing?

Honey Boy invented the space between that would later make Count Basie famous. That space between created opportunity. Opportunity lingered up into the open cedar rafters of the hall. A new century and a new era dawned; Jim Crow was still alive and well, but so was Honey Boy and so was the Funky Butt Jass Club and Storyville and New Orléans and Jass—America's classical and popular and dance music all in one. Jass was a music played with instruments from Europe to a beat from Africa for dancers everywhere. Jass was born in the fields from hollers, juke joint blues, and even the holy gospel of Honey Boy's beloved mother.

The purpose of life, son, is to be happy and to let others be happy. Everyone wants to be happy from the day they are born to the day they die, everywhere they go.

The most successful men of Storyville were not in the music business; they were in the sex and alcohol business. Music was just background, and most musicians worked day jobs to make ends meet. Honey Boy understood this and was at ease with it. He did not love money, nor did money love him. Honey Boy loved the scene, creating it, and enjoying it—smack dab in the middle of it. Honey Boy could create a scene and keep it interesting all night long, with or without the alcohol, but the sex was always present or, at least, imminent.

Bessie caught the eye of a short but muscular and well-dressed mustachioed sharecrop-slavery escapee who moved with the confidence he developed as a winning jockey. She beguiled him with a dipping of her head, a wink of both eyes, and a purposeful placing of her hand on her hip.

Bessie whispered a brag to Zora, "He's all mine now."

Sydney had ridden his former master's prize Tennessee Walker to freedom and opportunity; he intended to capitalize on his freedom and take advantage of this opportunity to court a sophisticated woman of the city, one who spoke Spanish or Italian…or French, preferably French. Bessie did, in fact, speak French, not well, but Sydney, who had stolen his former master's first name with his first horse, did not know the difference, much less care.

"Be careful," Zora warned.

Upon asking Bessie if she cared to dance at 11:55 p.m., her "*maís, oui*" in response was as sweet a sound to Sydney as the dulcet tones of Honey Boy's horn.

Zora watched Bessie and Sydney as the two locked eyes, then arms, then desires. It was almost midnight; waiting for the "double G" and love, Zora's envy drove her mind to wander.

If anyone knows what drove Honey Boy to wander off a parade procession into the arms of his cheering mother seven months later, they have remained silent, as silent as thereafter did Honey Boy's big horn and big-four beat that started it all with the big noise at the Funky Butt Jass Club.

Honey Boy had not appeared this night, with or without his 'Double G'. Instead, he was at home with mother celebrating grandmother's 69th birthday.

Tomorrow.

New Year's Eve.

That would be the night.

New Year's Eve 1906.

'Double G'

Hoodoo Lady

"He's a Voodoo Child."

"And you're a jealous fool."

"He can't play Storyville ever more, it's bad, bad, bad voodoo." Little David cleared his throat as he considered his audience. "No one's safe with Honey Boy playin' that voodoo music!"

"You play Jass, too," said Ethel.

"The Hell, you say, Hoodoo Lady; I invented Jazz, but no one plays music like that boy 'less they seen the Devil. 'sides he plays Boleros…in Spanish, and that ain't Jazz."

The Spanish, in fact, had barely missed being the first to colonize New Orléans during Spain's silver-and-gold crusade that drew them into Mexico and Peru. Alonso Álvarez de Pineda mapped and explored his way from Florida to Veracruz and noted the abundance of fresh water entering the Gulf in 1519. He hypothesized the existence of a large river; *Río de Espíritu Santo* Pineda named it after the Holy Spirit who created this marvel that Pineda never actually located. Ironically, though, the Spanish later left their mark in New Orléans later when Thomas Jefferson persuaded the banks, government, and citizens to use silver pesos as the currency of the day. Just as the pesos flowed in and around from Spain, the silver flowed back to Seville on the natural Gulf

Stream, which ushered sailors straight to Spain right out of Havana.

"Doesn't your uncle in Havana sing in Spanish?"

"Who's the fool now, woman? He plays in a Rumba outfit. Nothin' Jazz about it. Just fix him a hex, and let's be done with him."

"I do potions, not hexes."

It was actually Julia Jackson, cross-eyed and six feet tall, who practiced bad voodoo in the District. She claimed to have powers to cause abortion, induce pregnancy, infect with venereal disease, and even seal a woman up. The "sealing up" would prevent a strumpet from indulging a customer. So legendary were Julia's powers that scores of madams banded together in a benevolent society to draft a pact promising not to enlist the powers of voodoo on each other's business interests. Some also commissioned Eulalie Echo, godmother of Jelly Roll Morton, to counteract bad voodoo with good. And Zozo la Brique made a handsome profit selling brick dust to District dwellers to scrub away evil from their very doorsteps.

"Sister Ethel, You put a hex on old Deacon Jones, and he died the next day."

"I gave his wife a love potion, 'number three,' she was trying to steal him back from his girl. It didn't work, so she added some arsenic to it. He was old, anyway."

"Fine, give me some arsenic potion, then."

"I don't have any; you'd have to talk to Widow Jones. I want no part of this evil sorcery, anyway, I know Mother Golden; she's a good woman, a wise woman."

Every time we suffer, we can look around to see our brothers and sisters suffer. And when we look around, we can see that this is the way, the way of life, the human way. So, every time we overcome, we strengthen our mind, we lift our soul—closer to the Heavens.

"Stella? She's the cause of it all with her Buddha; now that woman is into some sorcery, alright. She's so evil the Lord struck her deaf and dumb—she's always scribblin' those damn notes that no one can understand. No good can come of a boy with a mother like that. Help me clean up this, this...boy wonder, the one who started it all!

Jump and shout

Holler and scream

Dust your pants, but

Don't bust a seam

"No."

"He was born under a full moon, from an evil woman, that's a bad sign."

"His mother is not evil or deaf. She just chooses not to talk with you or anyone else but her mother and her son, who was born on the Fourth of July, the moon had nothin' to do with it. "

"There was shootin' and hollerin' and discontent…"

"It was the Fourth of July…there's always shootin' and hollerin'."

"He was raised down in the Battlefield on the alley behind Perdido, nothin' good ever came out of that place."

"I seen you down there plenty with your gamblin' and your panderin'."

"Never mind, I'll get my girls to do it."

Little David was a quadroon—one-fourth black—Creole. He claimed that all his ancestors were French, which was almost true, given that France had colonized several areas of the West Africa of the forebears of Little David. He played piano and pimped at Jasmine's Sporting House in Storyville. He never received as many tips as any of the bar girls, like Bessie and Zora, but he somehow always had more money in his pocket than his 50-cent a day salary should allow. Little David left Ethel's just before dusk. He walked the roads less traveled, as he preferred, over to Jasmine's on North Basin Street.

Sydney escorted Bessie up the block, but stopped two doors down from Jasmine's, so as not to attract attention or draw the ire of Jasmine. Little David rounded the corner, walked up from behind the new couple and gawked as he passed them. Zora watched from the window of the sporting house and kept an eye out for the not-so-kindly matron. Little David loitered at the stoop, waiting to have a word with Bessie after she bade her new beau *"au revoir."*

Little David wasted no more time, "Where's Zora, I have some business for you two."

"What kind of business?"

"Lu-cra-tive."

"For you, or me?" Bessie knew to be skeptical of David's schemes. They were always sounded so simple and harmless, but often ended badly—for everyone.

"All three: you, Zora, and me."

Bessie waved up at Zora and motioned for her to join the business plan. Zora looked over one shoulder, then the other before stealing away, out the door, and down on the stoop. "Come on down, Princess Zora."

"What's this?" Zora asked Bessie.

"Little David here has a big plan for us, or so he says."

Zora rolled her eyes. "Count me out, last time David had a big plan we got lost 'cross town and missed our morning class."

"This will be as neat as paint." Little David assured the two as he put his arms around their shoulders and escorted them up the stairs and into the salon. He sat at the piano, bounced a rag, and vamped his plan:

All ya have to do

All ya have to do

Take a man

A drink or two

A bottle or two

A bottle or two

That's all

You

Have

to

Do

"A drink, or a bottle?" asked Bessie.

"So you'll do it?"

"It matters when…where…and what man."

"I so enjoy negotiating with you, Bessie, you are all business."

Zora watched on in apprehension. "Count me out I said."

Little David fingered an arpeggio to accent each answer.

"Tomorrow…Natchez…Our Wondrous Honey Boy Golden."

Zora and Bessie looked at each other for a moment.

"Count me out," said Zora.

"Wait, how much," asked Bessie.

Little David fingered three more arpeggios:

"Five…Dollars…Each."

Bessie and Zora looked at each other again, each hoping the other wouldn't say anything to queer the deal.

"Why Natchez, though, Zora and I saw him in town last night."

"He'll be at the Rhythm Club in Natchez tomorrow, trust me." Little David sealed the deal with a knowing glance at each of his errand girls.

"When do we get paid, and who's buying the steamboat tickets?" Bessie continued her negotiations.

"I'll have your tickets, your directions, and your bottles ready before you leave Jasmine's tonight."

Jasmine's was only one of over a dozen sporting houses on South Basin Street. Bienville Street boasted Fanny Gold's and 24 others; Iberville Street hosted the most, with Flo Meeker's and 31 others. Shrewd bawd Emma Johnson ran the largest house, which some referred to as a "circus." The three-and-half story building was an auditorium of carnal lust just down the street from Jasmine's. Altogether, the many houses of "the district" employed over 2000 prostitutes just after the turn of the century. The bar girls were not registered nor counted.

"Bottles?" Zora began to wonder aloud until Bessie shut her down with a warning scowl. Bessie ushered Zora upstairs to ready for the evening. "Stop pulling on me," Zora complained, "I don't trust him. Why doesn't he take the bottles himself?"

Little David slipped out the back door and over to Lafayette Street to Galloway's Barbershop. As he opened the door, Little David asked, "anyone seen Honey Boy?"

"He went to Natchez to play the Rhythm Club," Galloway said, "Aren't you the one who got him the gig?"

Little David smiled, "How about Tom Jones, he been around?"

"He's over at the Mandella's." Galloway replied. Little David hurried over to Mandella's grocery store on Liberty. He found Widow Jones' brother at the counter. "Tom, we need some help over at Jasmine's with some rats in the cellar, you got anything?"

"Sure, I got a tone of arsenic left from the Union Army munitions dump."

"How much would I need to kill a hundred rats?"

"You got a hundred rats at Jasmine's?"

"Maybe, but don't spread it around, it'd be bad for business."

"You probably need about a pound dry, or a spoonful if you put it is their drinking water."

"Fine, how much you want for two spoonsful?"

"Two dollars, plus delivery charge and application charge."

"Oh, I'll come pick it up now and mix it up in the water myself."

"Okay, but don't breathe it or accidentally drink any of it, it'll kill ya dead."

"Right," Little David assured Jones as the two walked over to Jones' house for the poison. On the way, they stopped by Pearl's Pool Hall for Little David to scout for any out-of-towners he could shark. Everyone in town knew better than to bet on a game against Little David. Unfortunately for Little David, the only patrons were regulars, one of whom was Big Bill Black. Little David slipped out of view quickly before Big Bill Black noticed him. Little

David regularly carried a .38 in his sock. Big Bill Black carried a Colt .45, brass knuckles, a bowie knife, and a chip on his shoulder for Little David, who had hustled him in more than a few games of pool. Big Bill Black still owed Little David $20 from that encounter, but that's not the way Big Bill Black saw it. As far as Big Bill Black was concerned, Little David still owed him the $200 Big Bill Black was up on the third game, before Little David ran the table on him, twice.

Ready for the evening, Bessie and Zora descended the stairway to the parlor to await the "gentlemen." Most of the men were gentle, but hardly gentlemen. There were butchers, bakers, soldiers, preachers, constables, bankers, and judges—all the men had one thing in mind: women. The bar girls and working girls had all manner of things on their minds, anything to transcend the bane of existence as a disposable object of desire. The girls were less than human to the men; to the girls, the men were nothing more than customers.

Little David and Jones reached the outhouse where Jones stored his alchemy materiel. Jones opened the door; the stench was staggering—a putrid mix of feces, urine, menstrual blood, sulfur, and the potassium nitrate that Jones sold as rat poison or composting agent.

"Smells like the devil, but it'll dissolve a tree stump in a week, and kill a dozen rats overnight," Jones bragged.

"Is this the same stuff we put in those Coca-Cola bottles?" asked David.

"No, no, no, that was just salt. If we had put this in, it woulda killed all our patients."

One boy in Oxnard had, in fact, died shortly after consuming the Coca-Cola and salt concoction that Jones and Little David were selling door to door as a cure for consumption. The two left California on the first freight train running to evade that scrape.

"That boy died of consumption, we just got to him too late. He was a lost cause." Jones said, half believing himself and half questioning himself. "Cola and salt has curative properties—we shoulda added some ginger like the Chinese. Ginger is good for anything. You never see Chinese with consumption."

"What about Old Mister Kim?" asked David.

"Kim, he was Korean; he died of heebie-jeebies, not consumption."

Little Dave grew impatient: "Heebie-jeebies? That's a dance, not a dis-ease—"

"He had a broken heart, anyway." Jones interrupted. "His wife left him for an Irish cop. You know how those fat Irish guys love little black-haired women."

Ethel tidied her parlor as she waited for her best customer, Sergeant Hill of the New Orléans Police, who paid her his top ill-gotten dollar for her love potion "Number Nine," which he used liberally on his octaroon mistress way across town.

A Spear and a Raid

Honey Boy squinted through the smoke, sized up the crowd as he wiped the sweat from the back of his neck, and smiled as he brought his cornet to his lips for another crowd-pleaser.

Honey Boy was actually undecided as to whether or not he would try to hit "double-G" this night. Maybe he wasn't ready.

"I got you a gig in Natchez," Little David told Honey Boy the day before.

"Thanks," Honey Boy looked into David's eyes, wondering, but not asking, why David didn't take the gig himself.

Maybe he should save it for next week up river. Little David had arranged Honey a two week engagement at The Rhythm Club with room and board. Honey Boy could try his chops in a smaller venue first. The "double-G" would make his name—but in a bad way if he tried and failed.

"We're countin' down to midnight, friends. Honey Boy was pacing the crowd, the band, and himself. "Soon it will be 1906, and let me be the first to say, 'Happy new year'!"

The spear that first pierced and then fell from the Rosewood wall heralded the entry of New Orléans' finest. They really weren't, the finest, nor did they exemplify much of anything at all. It was just a decent job with low official pay but opportunity to supplement the salary with "contributions" from "thankful" businessmen, working girls, and other major and minor criminals.

No one reached for his hat, as all still wore them, anticipating the well-known raid. The raid was necessary to keep the contributions coming. Establishments that could afford to "protect" their patrons contributed for the freedom from the raids. Establishments that could not afford such freedom experienced the raid as examples of what might happen to the others but for their contributions. Only a few patrons of the Funky Butt Jass Club contributed their way out of the paddy wagon. The rest would be out at 9 the next morning after a routine appearance before the magistrate and the imposition of a fine that they would not likely ever pay, except perhaps through coerced false testimony against a neighbor if the police needed a material witness to an otherwise unsolvable crime against a fairer citizen. The late night dancers would return home or to the farm or field for breakfast and family as usual.

It was not for respect but superstition that the police let the King of Storyville go free. Wouldn't it would be bad luck to arrest the one who started it all?

Farmer's in the city

Cow's in the meadow

Goat's in the corn

Let's dance in the ghetto

Mr. Honey Boy had not hit "double G" before or after midnight
that New Year's Eve but he was already at home well before
sunrise to begin 1906 with family. Mother Golden was proud,
strong, smart, and gentle. She raised her son so sweetly that no
one could even remember his real given name. Mrs. Golden had
called him "Honey Boy" so long it was all anyone ever knew to
call him. She did not talk often, instead regularly leaving her son
notes in his clothes' pockets.

*Serenity is ours to have, if we live for others as we live for
ourselves, if we show love for our brothers and sisters and aid
them in their times of need. When we share our strength, our
strength grows.*

Mrs. Golden baked for their living until Honey Boy was ten
and surpassed mother's earnings with his own from playing for
crowds who gathered around the prodigy to discern the trick
behind the impossibly talented young man. Most assumed a
ventriloquism act with a hidden adult musician behind a door
playing the notes while the diminutive street performer mimed the
sound. Eventually, though, older musician's joined the boy genius,
"Little Mozart" one called him, to create a new sound, distinctly

American and like nothing come before. Even European traditional dance music was barely recognizable with the simple but profound variations and style that Honey Boy brought to the classics. The big horn of the little man breathed new life into waltzes composed more than a century before his conception. There were regulars, but the band was informal on the streets in the day and afternoons. One day may feature a second cornet, a viola, a trombone, and a tuba; the next day maybe only a guitar and banjo accompanied Honey Boy. The night ensembles were strictly regulated, though, as the proprietors would only pay the official three members of the contracted band. The pay was decent for a few hours' work, but all the more so with the usual booty of tips: some in money, some in food, some in booze, some in flesh.

No one in town, except Mother, knew Honey Boy's father, or even what his name had been. There were rumors that he had been a famous French classical conductor who met Mother at the Opera House, but it made little sense since no one could explain how the very black woman could gain entry to the very white venue (except as a baker delivering goods).

Honey Boy himself told several stories about who his father was; sometimes a sea captain, sometimes a preacher, sometimes a Civil War hero for the Union. Many later claimed to have fathered Honey Boy after his fame, but there were too many to begin to investigate. Mother, for her part, was not talking. Father Golden, in fact, was a man of peace, a man of the sea, a man of war, and a man of God; he was a retired United States Navy chaplain. And although there was much love between his parents, alack, it was not to be. Father Golden, who went by another surname, had chosen another for his bride, not knowing of the conception of his son. Soon thereafter, the chaplain was reported lost at sea with his ship that was on pirate patrol in the Caribbean. In his teens Honey

Boy settled on calling his father "Aman Rey," after the Egyptian god of sun. When they finally met, Honey Boy learned he was right.

Father Golden, in fact, had been something of a Civil War hero for the Union. He served Commodore Collins as a scout. Father, then First Mate, Golden once ran 13 miles ahead of Collins' marines and 13 miles back in order to alert the commodore of the advance of Confederate troops and the flanking of Cherokee braves. Collins sent the first mate to negotiate a truce with the Cherokees while his troops flanked the rebels on the opposite side just long enough to distract them from the ultimately successful frontal assault. First Mate Golden shot not and fought not, but made the victory possible by his indefatigable efforts as spy and ambassador. These feats won him a battlefield commission and promotion to ensign.

The French Governor of the Louisiana Colony during the French and Indian Wars, Louis Billouart, Chevalier de Kerlerec, or *Chef Menteur* as the Choctaws named him for his dishonesty, more feared attacks from Cherokees than from the British Navy, which never entered the French garrison at New Orléans. The French troops availed themselves, throughout the 1750s, of the bars and brothels while they awaited a British invasion that never materialized except as a blockade of the Gulf of Mexico that prevented any French ship from entering the Mississippi for over four years. Louis XV, in a secret deal, ceded Louisiana to Spain just before negotiating peace with Britain. Spanish governance developed an organized city of New Orléans to include over 100 drummers and fifers as well as official town criers and trumpeters to play reveille each morning and taps each night during the 1770s.

"God made you wonderful, and you make this world wonderful with your works, and your work is your music; you bless us all," Abyssinian Red inspired by personal sermon. In lieu of his father, the street preacher, philosopher, and blues singer regularly advised Honey Boy on issues of morality and practicality. Honey Boy gradually came to believe that he was wonderful and that his music was a gift, one that he must share. "God gave you so that you may share," Red urged.

Red lived in the janitor's closet at Fisk School in the heart of Storyville at Franklin and Perdido, where his godfather was the janitor. When Red wasn't on the street corner singing and preaching, he was listening to the teachers and their lectures. Fisk purveyed enlightenment and morality in the midst of the bars and brothels of Storyville. Fortunately for the teachers and the students, the neighborhood was relatively quiet during school hours, and the residents were quite proud of their school.

Red had attended Fisk as a child, even after he went blind at age six. He returned at age seven, recovered from his illness and longing for acceptance and purpose. The head teacher, Enrico Miguel, was the son of Cuban parents who came to New Orléans as travelling musicians. Miguel was determined to find, or make, a place for Red at Fisk. Miguel first had Red hand out pencils and erasers to children who came by the school office. Next, after Red learned to navigate the halls and rooms by memory and touch, Miguel had Red carry messages to teachers in the classrooms. Then, Miguel asked the janitor to teach Red to sweep and mop, which went well for all. Last, and most successfully, upon the suggestion of Miguel's mother, Miguel's father taught Red to play guitar. Miguel had to take the guitar away from Red several times that first year after Red played his fingers raw to bleeding.

Miguel's mother then taught Red to sing rumbas and *son*. *Son* came to Havana with Miguel's parents at the end of the 19ᵗʰ century bringing the African beat of the country to the Iberian claves of the city. Mother Miguel taught Red to sing not from his mouth, throat, diaphragm, or heart. She taught Red to sing from his *alma*. Red's soul was deep and pure as was his music. At first the other children ignored Red, then mocked him, later tolerated him, eventually adored him, and ultimately missed him when Miguel's replacement forbade Red from singing at lunch in the cafeteria because of "safety" concerns. Red turned to the streets then, at fifteen, and began singing for change. Passersby often enjoyed Red, occasionally tipped him, and rarely robbed him. Red made enough money to survive. On the street, though, he more than survived—he thrived.

Red thrived on humanity.

Although everyone knew Red's father, the accomplished dancer, no one in The District knew Red's mother. Red had one memory but no photos of his mother. He could always picture in his mind's eye his mother's bright red hair and beaming white smile as she pushed him on the swing at the park. He was three. She smelled like vanilla and peaches. Her voice still rang in his ears like a birdsong. Red did not remember, but it was in Tampa, Florida. Dad left when mom died. Little Red didn't travel well to New Orléans; he had developed glaucoma. His sight darkened and constricted every day in his first year at Fisk. Red prayed every night. Red's father took Red to no fewer than eleven doctors—so called. By the end of first grade Red was nearly blind. He did not start second grade. Red cried every day…until Dad put him back in school after Christmas break.

Red was completely blind.

Red's classmates at first refused to believe that Red was blind, thinking it was all some sort of practical joke. After a few quiet lectures from teachers, though, the Fisk student body came to accept the reality of their fellow. By spring they had forgotten all about it and went on with the joys of play and childhood. Red became just another playmate, as he had been. The adults kept an eye on Red, while the children soon forgot about his blindness and played with him as before. Dominoes was Red's favorite game; he could readily feel the dots and easily play just as before. Red also still loved the swings. He would swing and sing the songs his mother sang to him: lullabies from Ireland. He even feigned a brogue. It was then that Miguel first noticed Red's talent for music. Red taught Miguel Irish lullabies and Miguel taught Red Cuban boleros.

Red sat in on most of his regular class time and tried his best to learn by hearing, which he did well. His memory became legend. Eventually other children came to Red to ask his memories on what others had said; the children accepted Red's memories as gospel. No one questioned Red's version of past conversations, statements, or promises, no matter how significant or trivial.

David was the runt of the class. He used his sense of humor, his cunning, and cash to make his way. Little David realized the value of Red's talent and legend, so David determined to capitalize on both. Red summarily rejected David's first proposals to say sooth or cast spells.

"You're like an oracle, Red…why not make some money off that?" David beamed.

Red was leery of David's scheme: "How am I an oracle? I can barely put my clothes on in the morning."

"All the kids trust you; you could tell them anything about their future and they'd just believe you. We could make piles and piles of money off that."

"Who has money here?"

"Trust me, they'll find money to pay to know what their future holds."

"How would I know? I'm just a kid."

"Doesn't matter," David tried to close the deal, "just tell 'em what they want to hear: they'll be 'rich,' they'll be 'happy,' they'll have 'lots of friends,' they'll 'marry into royalty'…they'll have 'lots of kids and a big house on the river…up in Natchez'…" "What if it never comes true?"

"Simple, how will they know? By the time they know whether or not it's true, we already got and spent their money."

"Why you keep sayin' we? What are *you* gonna do?"

"I'll bring in the suckers," Little David whispered, nudging Red. Little David continued his pitch unabashed.

Red remained unconvinced. "Then what?"

"You just tell them all the good stuff."

Red found the plan unrealistic and unappealing, but he had his own plan. "Why don't I just sing them a happy song?"

Little David was incredulous, "What?"

"I'll just sing them a happy song, like a lullaby…like moms sing."

"A lullaby? Who's gonna pay for that?"

"I you're so smart, you tell me. Or you just tell them. Tell 'em that if I sing them a happy song that the happy stuff will all come true." Red smiled sincerely.

Little David pondered, then agreed reluctantly. "Yeah, yeah, we could do that. 50-50, deal?"

Red hesitated. "Deal."

And so began Red's career as a professional musician.

Little David's career as a con man, on the other hand, had already begun. The year prior, at the age of eight, David sold, door to door, bibles he had stolen from neighborhood churches.

To See God

"I want to see God."

"Surely you will, when your time is come, Honey Boy," Red assured his surrogate son.

"I want to see him and come back here to tell you what he looks like," said Honey Boy.

"Well, I've been blind since I was six, Honey Boy, but I'll see God in my own way and on the day of his choosing."

"I'm thirteen now, I'm a man, and I'm ready to see God," Honey Boy proclaimed.

"No gospel of mortals he preaches this boy, but the gospel of the Lord himself, Galatians 1:12." Red plucked the strings of his beaten old dreadnought guitar with its blonde spruce top and hole where a pick guard should be. Red grew the nails on his right hand long enough to strum the steel strings without a pick. He would down-strum with his thumb on the bass strings and up strum with his fingernails on the high four strings. He didn't play fancy, but it somehow sounded as though two were playing rather than one. Red improvised a song for the occasion:

There was a boy

A wondrous boy

Said he wanted to see

The Holy Father

Yes indeed, yes indeed

And what would he do

If he did see?

"I'd play him my best song," said Honey Boy.

"Your best song, and what would that be, 'Honey Boy Blues'?"

"No, I got a new one, wrote it last night under the full moon, so I call it 'Full Moon Serenade'."

A cascade of triplets sang through the dusk of the Storyville sunset as Honey Boy Golden played, for the first time in public, the song that made him a man, the song that made him an artist, the song that would make him a legend.

Neither Red nor anyone else who had a foot could resist tapping it when Honey Boy played his "Full Moon Serenade," nor could anyone who danced sit still, nor could anyone who daydreamed resist reverie. It was a timeless piece that celebrated what it meant to be alive in the fullest sense of what W.E.B. Du Bois might call "humanity." The song was breath and light and creation itself. Within a decade, when Honey Boy no longer played aloud, gypsy jazz bands in Paris, ragtime piano players in San Francisco, woodwind ensembles in St. Petersburg, and tango orchestras in Buenos Aires each offered their audiences their own versions of Honey Boy Golden's "Full Moon Serenade."

Red sat in silence for a while.

"Well, what do you think. What would God say?"

"I don't know" was all Red could say.

Red later found another musician who called himself "Cornelius Robespierre" to transcribe the song and give Honey Boy credit for the composition. As was common for the day, somehow neither ever saw more than $100 of royalties for the sheet music that sold millions of copies. This or that agent or lawyer or distributor or publisher always had a reason not pay their share. Worse yet, the one who started it all never recorded the song himself, nor did he ever record any song—that survived.

Though it was never recorded by its originator; not Red, nor anyone else, would ever forget the first time they heard "Full Moon Serenade."

Shimmy down

Shake me up

Come around and

Fill my cup

Honey Boy was a standout at church, first in his manners, then in his voice. As a young child, he would stand between his mother and grandmother and chant out the hymns from heart and memory, not always understanding the words but always in key and on time. Everyone knew the Goldens by good name and reputation. They were Christians, yes indeed, good God-fearin' Baptists of the Southern order. When he turned ten, Honey Boy auditioned for the choir. By then he had memorized the words to 137 hymns, several for each season and occasion. The performance became a sort of entertainment with the pianist trying to stump the prodigy by playing hymns not sung in church for several months. After 21 challenges, the wondrous boy had earned his place: first tenor.

Mother and grandmother ran a bakery out of their home, or rather they made a home out of their bakery. There was no sign in the window, on the door, or hanging outside, but everyone called it simply "Alley Bakery." To Honey Boy the smell of the yeasty rising and baking bread meant home. He would wake each morning to a warm room overflowing with the delightful aromas of egg bread, cross buns, and cinnamon rolls. The heat waved in the air as it rose off the ovens and steamed the windows with yeasty condensation. The Jews in neighboring districts would walk a mile or more on Saturday for the Alley Bakery's challah. Honey Boy would play quick games of hide-and-seek with dusty Jewish boys and girls who had not yet met Jim Crow.

By age 11, Honey Boy began playing cornet with adults at picnics, parks, advertisements, and afternoon dances. A promoter once invited him to play in a hot air balloon hovering over a political rally, but Mother Golden would hear none of it.

Nature cherishes love and compassion above all else. Politics knows neither, son. The politician is interested primarily in himself. When he is old and ill, all the power in the world will mean nothing. All the politician will want on his deathbed is compassion.

Storyville was a tough place to raise children, but it was not without compassion, albeit in spite of all the nocturnal goings-on. In an almost unnoticed antithesis to segregation, white Jews in "the District" lived alongside yellow Chinese, black Africans, brown Cubans, and red Chahtas, some of whom would later become the "Wild Tchoupitoulas," famous for their home-made extravagant Mardi-Gras costumes. Chinese restaurants in Storyville added red

beans to their rice on menus to appeal to local palettes. Anti-
Semitism in the country created a sympathy in many Jews for the
anti-African-American sentiments rampant throughout the South.
Despite the racism, segregation, vice, and violence, there were
plenty of children in Storyville, though.

Honey Boy didn't have much time for fun and games as a
child, though, he was too busy with his music. His first instrument
was a harmonica. He played it like a drum—it was strictly a
rhythm instrument. Honey Boy mimicked the hypnotic other-
world beats that bounced through Storyville from Congo Square.

The Sunday afternoon rhythms pulsing from the Square came
straight out of Africa. The afternoons were part music, part dance,
part concert, and part worship. There was always community, too.
Some traditions continued there included women circling a
drummer and dancing in what many later called a "Conga line."
The beats pounded out from small drums, long drums, round
drums, and square drums. Some were wood, other animal skins;
some drummers beat their rhythms with sticks, others with their
hands, and some even with their feet. The Eighteenth and
Nineteenth Century European onlookers found these events
"savage," "uncouth," or "mischievious," but the Europeans
watched them just the same. Sometimes musicians accompanied
the drums on stringed instruments, sometimes with voice,
sometimes only with stomps.

By age twelve Honey Boy had already written seven original
songs: two blues, two rumbas, two 32-bar jazz choruses, and one

bolero. He wrote the songs first in his mind while he lay in bed at night with his eyes open staring out his window at the stars and trying to see Heaven. He heard lyrics, felt rhythms, and imagined chord progressions. The melodies mused next, as pure inspiration.

"Where do you derive your music?" asked Cantor Levi.

"It just comes to me." And they kept coming, sometimes a new song every day, sometimes two songs in one day, and each more joyous than the next.

Professor Jackson taught standard music notation at Fisk. Honey Boy learned to read notes in second grade and went home over the summer to start playing with re-writing the notes to songs he had learned at school. The next summer he was writing notes to songs he learned by ear on the street. And the summer after that he was writing notes to songs he heard in his head. Each September Professor Jackson greeted his star pupil with genuine enthusiasm and awe in discovering what new talent Honey Boy had developed since June.

"What have you now, young buck?" asked Professor.

"I wrote a blues and a bolero."

"Let us hear, let us hear."

Honey Boy counted himself in: "two, three, four," and played his blues like a man, a wise man, a soulful man.

"Yes," said Professor in approval, "those are the blues."

"I call it 'Honey Boy Blues'."

"I can feel it."

"Is it good?"

"It's better than good, son, it's hot and sweet—both, at the same time…"

"Thanks." Honey Boy half-understood but fully-appreciated the praise, especially considering the source. He wasn't sure if he should share it with Mother Golden. What if she doesn't like "hot and sweet" music? What if she just wanted her precious son to play "The Lord's sacred music?"

All the way home, Honey Boy pondered.

"Is hot and sweet music good music, Red?"

"The best"

"But is it the Lord's sacred music?"

"The Lord wouldn't want your music to be any more sacred than hot and sweet."

"But will my mother think so?"

"Oh, now, I think you could persuade her if you just play her some of those sweet and hot notes, Honey Boy."

"What if she doesn't like it?"

"She will, she will."

"But if she doesn't, what will I do? I won't be able to play it anymore."

Honey Boy opened the door slowly and quietly.

"Is that you, Honey Boy?"

"It's me, Gramma, is mom home?"

"She's at the market. Just you and gramma."

"Do you like sweet music, gramma?"

"Yes I do—it gives me peace."

"How about hot music?"

"When I want to dance, there's none better."

"Does Mother like it?"

"Your mother loves your music, Honey Boy."

"But is it 'Lord's Sacred Music'?"

"Well, it may not be church music, but people aren't always in church, are they? If people sing the gospel on Sunday and cabaret on Monday, that pleases the Lord just fine."

"What about Mother?"

"Your Mother is too good-hearted to judge people's hot and sweet music, Honey Boy. Don't you worry your pretty little head for one second about that gift the Lord gave you. The Lord loves your music and so does your mother—you can be sure of it."

Honey Boy was not so sure. He went up in his loft to read the Bible until Mother returned. Honey Boy soon fell asleep. He dreamt of flowers, dancers, parades, and honey—all in the brightest colors. The flowers smelled as happy as sunshine. They waved gently in a breeze beneath the dancers who strutted and pranced as light as angels. The parades blared triumphant down the streets, joyous humanity in motion defying gravity by walking on the sides of buildings, then up their walls, then over their roofs. The honey dripped onto his tongue magically from a floating hive, never tasting better, just so sweet, but not too—just right. Then

Honey Boy was leading the parade. The dancers lifted him high above the crowds up into the clouds and finally into Heaven. Honey Boy did not see the Lord, but he knew the Lord was there. He played his cornet all the sweeter for the honey on his lips; he played his music all the hotter for the joy in his heart; he felt the Lord's love as never before.

"Gramma, gramma!" Honey Boy rejoiced upon waking.

"Yes?" Grandmother called.

"The Lord…he loves my music…he loves it…he loves it!"

"The Lord loves your music most of all, Honey Boy."

Just then, Mother Golden returned home with eggs, flour, cinnamon, sugar, and nutmeg. She looked first at Grandma, then at Honey Boy and knew better than to pry. They were both happy; Mother Golden was happy—they were all happy. They were together and they were happy. The Lord loved them, yes indeed, the Lord loved each and all.

We need love for our very foundations. We all depend on each other. It matters not at all how skillful we are; we can only thrive together, not alone.

Just Bee

Walking to market with grandmother and aunt, Beatrice in her cream shirtwaist caught the mind's eye of all who beheld her youthful beauty. She went by "just Bee" and in all times and all ways was the goodness of graciousness. Beyond good, she was the best of good, the kind of girl who inspired righteousness and humility in the hardest of souls. It was Christmas Eve 1902 and unseasonably warm. She had heard "the wondrous boy" play his cornet twice prior, but this time she appreciated it in a way that she never had before. At fourteen, she was a year older than Honey Boy and would remain taller for three years. She had strong arms from carrying goods and siblings. Her glowing black locks bounced with a buoyant loose curl that radiated calico colors in the sun. Her soft skin glistened with a sweet sweat that also moistened her brow. Her back swayed in a shallow "S" that marks a strong feminine health and beauty.

Her neck, though, was what caught Honey Boy's eye that day, but only for a glimpse. It was a glimpse that he would remember all his live long days, in sickness and in health. Her face was pretty and her figure alluring, but her neck…her neck…that neck…it should inspire a grand statue…or a song.

He wasn't sure if her eyes met his as she glanced over her shoulder before rounding the corner toward the market, but then he was mesmerized by that which held the head that held the eyes.

"What's your name?" He couldn't help but yell.

"Just Bee," she hollered back from around the corner without returning or even looking back.

As if offering a secret sign of a lover, she tossed a penny over her shoulder, and it rolled halfway toward Honey Boy.

"We can only truly learn after we truly love," said Red, hearing the penny roll down the street.

" 'Bee'? What kind of name is that?"

"Short for 'Beatrice,' son. That's a fine young girl, my boy. I can tell by her voice. She has the voice of an angel, an angel thrice blessed."

"Beatricia…Beatricia…Beatricia," Honey Boy muttered all the way home that day.

At home, a song came to Honey Boy, but not just *a* song, *the* song. He would play it only for her…after he played it for him.

"What is this new song today," asked Red.

"It's private, I'll never play it for anyone but her…and you…it's my '*Bolero Por Beatricia*'."

Spanish Governor Estevan Rodriguez Miró's Edicts of Good Government decreed that the *bailes de negros* be allowed on Sundays, but only after vespers. There had been complaints in the

1780s that some heathen Africans were dancing the *Bamboula* on Sabbath. Miro, oddly, referred to the dance as "*Los Tangos*" for some reason known only to him, but wisely and respectfully ensured their continuation. The dancing, then, long outlasted the edicts and Spanish rule. The "Spanish tinge," as Jelly Roll Morton would later call it, however, became an essential ingredient of American Jazz, and Argentine tangos were popular in New Orléans by 1920, before catching on in New York and Europe.

"Spanish, yes, now that's a language of love."

"No, no…no words, just music…it's too sweet for words."

Honey Boy played his new creation like a man, like an artist, like a lover. The sweet melancholy tones hung in the morning air like a velvet dress on a full-bodied young mother awaiting her tardy husband. The song was at once loving and longing; it was jealous—but not needy.

"I believe you just hit 'double F'," Red noted calmly but proudly, "but that sounds like a bolero, like Pepe Sanchez and his Trovadores. I heard your mother play Bizet's *Carmen* bolero once. She plays like a gypsy—used to."

The violins that came to the District from Italy were not dissimilar to a stringed Senegambian instrument from West Africa, but no matter how fancy or worn, when played in Storyville jazz outfits, it was strictly a "fiddle." Fiddles and banjos regularly inspired dancers indoors and out, day and night.

"She sold her violin," Honey Boy reminded Red.

"You ought to buy it back for her."

"What about Beatricia? How do I meet her?"

"She's a young woman, you're a young man, you are supposed to meet; you already have."

"So..."

"You will again."

Honey Boy rhapsodized an earthy Blues.

"D-minor, the saddest key."

His youth and innocence made the blues even bluer: more gut and more bucket. His nose flared, his brow perspired, his veins pulsed, and his loins ached. Wonder and lust consumed the wondrous boy, the one who started it all.

Take my hand

Tap your feet

Squeeze me hard

Down in the street

"But, but, but..."

"No time for *buts*, Honey Boy."

"But... I don't know what to do..."

"You don't need to know what to do; it will come to you at the time. This is the Lord's way. Let it be."

"Bee?"

"Let it be…"

"Bee…atricia, Beatricia, Beatricia."

"Sing your song, Honey Boy, she will return…in good time."

Bee sang at her mother's side all the way to the market six days a week. She sang once at the market, attracting customers for the jellies and jams she and her mother canned and sold. She danced a street ballet of sincerity and soulfulness that came not from study but from freedom.

Honey Boy imagined Beatricia's scent. Flowers. Powder. Peach.

Bee heard Honey Boy's voice in her mind from time to time and pictured his handsome face—part man, part cherub.

Honey Boy imagined the texture of her skin—the moist and smooth suppleness of her neck. He had never touched a girl's neck before, but he wanted to. He wanted to something fierce. He longed and ached just to touch Beatricia's ballerina neck.

Bee imagined the warmth of Honey Boy's hand holding hers as they walked through the grass on their way to the river for an afternoon swim.

Honey Boy could taste her sweet sweat dripping from her chin as he kissed it away. He had never kissed a girl before, but he wanted to. He wanted to something fierce. He longed and ached to kiss Beatricia's angel face.

Bee saw them as dolphins in the sea racing through the azure waters somewhere in the Caribbean outrunning all sharks and flying up above the surface into the air, splashing back down playfully. She imagined them as tigers in the jungle lumbering lazily through the triple canopy, fearing nothing.

Honey Boy lay awake each night playing his songs in his mind. Beatricia was there, always: in the front row at a concert…or the best table at a club…or sitting next to him in a rocking chair on the front porch of their very own country home.

Bee imagined the two as birds in the forest making a nest at the top of the highest tree on the ridge overlooking the rest of creation.

Bee created sculptures from anything she could find at home. Mud, clay, wax. Any hard or sharp object was a tool in her hands.

"Leonardo said men paint with their minds, not their hands," Bee's mother shared with her daughter, trying to inspire Bee.

"Well, I think I sculpt with my hands…and my heart. I'm a girl. Da Vinci is an old man."

Bee's mother could not help but laugh. "What are you making?"

"I don't know yet." Bee continued carving the wax candle cylinder the size of a bottle of wine.

"Who's it for?"

Bee stopped carving. "No one in particular."

"You're thirteen now and a beautiful girl, men are going to start taking an interest in you. You—"

"I am not interested in men."

"You will be, though, and you—"

"I will be interested in only one man."

"Oh, which man is this?"

"I don't know, Mother, but I will know when I meet him." Bee continued paring down the candle with the knife.

"It's starting to look like an angel…"

"An angel?"

"Why don't you sculpt an angel…we can give it to grandma to take with her to Heaven."

Bee tried to smile as her eyes drew tears. A single tear dropped onto the candle. Another dropped on Bee's left hand, which was still carving.

Wings.

A head.

A body.

A face. Eyes. Ears. Nostrils.

A beak.

"That's a lovely hummingbird, Bee."

"Maybe, but it's supposed to be a dove."

"Grandma would love it."

"Grandma doesn't like birds, she's scared of 'em." Bee thought of Honey Boy and how he might react if she gave him the sculpture as a gift.

"Well, we could sell it at market tomorr—"

"No, I'm not finished with it." Bee wrapped the wax dove in her mother's handkerchief and placed it in her keepsake box she then slid under her bed.

Bee walked over to Grandma who was asleep in her rocking chair in front of the fire. Bee took Grandma's hand and massaged it, stretching out each arthritic finger individually. Grandma awoke, smiled, then closed her eyes again. Bee massaged the other hand.

"Here's the brush." Mother handed Bee Grandma's favorite brush. Bee slowly unfurled Grandma's hair from its loose bun and brushed it methodically, gradually working up from the tips on each successive stroke.

Grandma begun humming "Blue Danube." Mother joined in.

"Grandma loves her waltzes," Mother reminisced.

"Johannes Sebastian Strauss." Bee guessed semi-correctly.

"Well, I don't think that was his middle name, but it was Strauss, very good, Bee." Mother was genuinely proud of her daughter.

"Tell me the story of Grandma at the Octaroon Ball," Bee entreated her mother."

"Oh," Mother began reluctantly, "The Octaroon Ball is not much to be proud of, sweetheart."

Bee walked in front of Grandma, took both her hands, and helped her to stand. "Show us how you dance, Grandma, show us who was the Belle of the Ball."

"The Belle of the Ball, the Belle of the Ball, that's me." Grandma's eyes opened slowly, then became bright in joy. Bee lead Grandma in a waltz box step in front of the fire. "Oh, come on, girl, your grandma can do more than a silly little box step. That's for old people who can't dance." Grandma elevated into perfect posture and levitated up onto her light feet. She lead Bee around the back of the rocking chair, over by the kitchen table, reversed direction, steered Bee to within one inch of Bee's bed in the opposite corner, steered Bee back to the center of their one room home, lead a full turn in place, and dipped Bee gracefully until Bee's hair almost touched the floor.

"Grandma, Grandma, don't drop—l"

"I got you," Mother rushed to the rescue.

"Oh, I could get you down, girl, but you're too heavy to pick up," Grandma laughed, "What you been eatin', concrete and lead?"

"Come on, Grandma," Mother ushered Grandma back to her rocking chair.

Grandma sat down slowly, her muscles quivering and her joints creaking. "Aaaahhh," she relaxed into her chair, stared into the fire, and returned to humming "Blue Danube."

"There she is, the Belle of the Ball," Bee complimented her grandmother.

"No, no, that was that mean old Jezebel from First Street, Leslie Cordianne. All the white men loved her; she was shameless hussy. She didn't even like men, though, just their money. She actually liked us girls. We called her Leslie the lezzy—she was lesbi—"

"Grandma, should we sing another song," Mother interrupted the impromptu sex education lesson.

"I don't care about lesbians, Grandma, tell me about your dress," Bee said.

"My dress? Oh, my dress was the prettiest thing you ever saw. My father was a tailor—best in town. He sewed all the costumes for the French Opera." Grandma looked down at her feet. "His brother made all the shoes—slippers too. Father took apart costumes that weren't gonna be used until next season and used the fabric on a dress for me—prettiest peach silk from Paris." Grandma raised her hands up to the sky. "Leslie said I looked like an angel. Then she kissed me—on the lips. I felt so—"

"Grandma, do you want something to—"

"Mother, stop interrupting," Bee interrupted her mother. "Go on, Grandma, how did you feel?"

"I felt weightless in those shoes…they were like Cinderella's magic slippers. I could have danced all night. Danced all night, Lord knows. We danced all night. All night…all night."

Grandma trailed off back into sleep, then mumbled in her dreams, "Dance…all night…all night…good Lord."

Mother's Violin

"I'll never see God until I return Mother's violin."

"Despair is the weakest sin," said Red.

"This is private, Red, it's not a public matter."

"Set aside your polemics, Honey Boy, and be a poet of peace. The violin has not found you, so you must seek it like a pilgrim seeks salvation."

"Who bought it? She won't tell me."

"You're moving in circles…go straight to and straight from, like a pilgrim."

"Who bought it?"

"Your father bought it for your mother when you were born. He bought you that cornet, too."

"You know my father?" Honey Boy felt flush.

"No, but your mother does, and she told me all about her golden maple violin and your brass cornet. Go ask Karnofsky."

"Karnofskfy?"

"A friend of your father."

Katrina Karnofsky was a brilliant portraitist. Oil, canvas, light, life. From her mind, her soul, her hands, two dimensions became three. Work became art. She had trained at the finest institute in St. Petersburg on a scholarship endowed by the Tsarina herself. Upon graduating, Karnofsky left the snows of Russia for the gold of California but settled in Louisiana after earning more money in a weekend on the streets of New Orléans than she had all her weekends sketching portraits for tourists in St. Petersburg.

Mother sold Karnofsky her golden maple violin for three good reasons. One, Karnofsky had cash and would part with it for a handsome instrument. Two, Karnofsky would never actually play the instrument or sell it to another. Three, Karnofsky would sell it back to her when Mother Golden was ready.

Karnofsky lived in a barn by the lake.

Lake Pontchartrain is actually not a lake but an estuary. It opens into the Rigolets channel on its way to another body of water, Lake Borgne, which is also an estuary. Lake Borgne receives fresh water from the Pearl River and mixes it with the tidal actions of the Gulf of Mexico in an area that was popular with the Canadian fur traders off season. The trappers worked only a few months a year at their trade and spent the rest of the year on other pursuits, including homesteading in Louisiana with their native-American brides, some of whose situations were probably better described as sex slavery than holy matrimony.

Karnofsky liked everything about her situation: the light, the mist, the solitude, the owl. Every once in a while a young couple would try to sneak in to frolic in the hay, but finding none in the barn come studio, they would soon leave for another lover's hideaway. So, mostly Karnofsky was alone, away from people so she could concentrate on her portraits, which the artist painted mostly from imagination. The work probably qualified as impressionistic, or perhaps expressionistic, but Karnofsky insisted that his art was "classic with color." Karnofsky pronounced this school and philosophy so matter-of-factly that no one questioned it. It didn't matter a whit, for an agent sold every piece for a handsome profit. Karnofsky never painted anyone famous except Rasputin, though they had never met, only heard of him. Karnofsky heard that the two were born on the same day and in the same village on the Tura River.

Most any person could view the portraits and see a relative or friend in the happy and healthy faces. In the end, Karnofsky painted joy, not people, and rich miserable customers in New York City, Philadelphia, and Detroit parted with small fortunes to bring color and joy into their otherwise dreary city homes.

The barn studio was a good half day's walk from the North Basin Street corner where the Wondrous Boy and Red squatted.

"Go on, then," Red encouraged. As Honey Boy gathered his belongings and counted his money, Red improvised:

Down by the lake

Out in a barn

The Russian artist

Has what you seek

Go now, don't tarry

Go now, go now

Bring back your

Family honor

Bring back your

Family treasure

Honey Boy knew the way to the Lake; he had walked it with his Mother and Gramma one Thanksgiving for a family reunion.

He walked it anew now. He walked it with hope; he walked it with wonder, not even realizing when he had walked past a King, or "Professor" as the District folk called him.

Tony "Professor" Jackson was an epileptic who drank just enough to calm his seizures but not enough to preclude him from holding forth as the "best blues player who ever lived," according to jazz critic and historian Clarence Williams. In the best of blues traditions, the Professor never played a song the same way twice. He was a master improviser and entertainer, packing every bar and brothel in Storyville night after night, year after year—wherever he held forth.

"In a hurry, young buck?" Professor Jackson asked, but Honey Boy just kept walking, not even registering the question. "I say," Professor said louder, "you too big now to stop and talk awhile?"

"Oh, say, Professor…I didn't even notice you there. I'm off to the lake…" Honey Boy broke his reverie.

"Karnofsky's?" Asked Professor Jackson.

"Yep, Red said she has my mother's violin."

"It's in safe hands, then—only Russian I know who can't play violin—helluva painter, though."

"Yes, yes, I heard."

"How will you make it back in time, don't you have a gig tonight?"

"No, not until day after tomorrow, up in Natchez."

"Natchez, how'd you get a gig up in Natchez?"

"Little David."

"Little David," Professor Jackson shook his head sternly, "Why would Little David get you a gig in Natchez, he despises you?"

Honey Boy was surprised by the Professor's statement, "What do you mean?"

"Jealousy is a very ugly thing, Honey Boy. Have you noticed how he's always trying to steal your best players from your band?"

"What, Little David plays with us…when you're not around."

"Sure, then at break, he's always tryin' to steal your musicians. He even tried to get me to play Independence Day Parade with him."

"But, why would he want two pianos in the same band?"

Professor Jackson shook his head in dismay. "He doesn't need two pianos, he just doesn't want you to have one."

"Well, it's three months away, I haven't even asked anyone yet." Nausea crept into Honey Boy..

"You better get your act together, son, call in your brothers, form your outfit before all the best are already booked."

Honey Boy's head filled with worries on the way out to the Lake: *Little David…Natchez…Independence Day Parade…best musicians…jealousy.* But they all passed once he finally saw the water, and Karnofsky's barn.

"Honorable welcome, no luvfer with you? asked Karnofsky, with a faint Russian accent while looking Honey Boy over from toe to head."

"No, no I'm looking for a special instrument." Honey Boy looked around the barn.

"Ah…yes an adventure, this is good…good for a young soul. Tell me then, what is your art, young soul?"

"Art?" Honey Boy was tired from the long walk.

"What do you create?"

"I play music"

"What type of music?"

"Jass."

"So, you are a poet?"

"Well, I write songs…"

"Good, good, songs, yes, the best use of a poem. Sing me a song, young soul." Honey Boy brought his cornet from his sack and just finished the introduction to "Full Moon Serenade" before Karnofsky interrupted: "I know your mother…Stella."

"Do you have her violin, I want to buy it back."

"No, your father has it."

Honey Boy inhaled slowly. Finally exhaling, he risked, "Do you know where he is?"

"Natchez…with the millionaires."

"Why is he up there? He's not a millionaire." Honey Boy's mind raced.

"Man can be a tragic beast, powerful yet fallible. Anything that ends in happiness is a comedy, though. Comedy is for the people, tragedy is for kings. You and your dad and me, we aren't important enough to be tragic. He's not a millionaire, no. He is too happy."

"How do you know he's happy?"

"His mind is in flight. He sails the river, just as he dreamed when he was your age. See this painting?" Karnofsky nodded her head pointing to a portrait of three ballerinas jumping across the stage. "This is flight, ballet is flight." Honey Boy walked slowly up to the portrait that was leaning against the barn wall propped up off the straw floor by three-dozen bricks forming a cradle for the four-foot by six-foot painting.

"It's beautiful." Honey Boy gazed at the portrait, mesmerized by the color and light.

"Three is the number of genius, the number of beauty. Beauty is the highest goal of art, and art is the ultimate product of the human being. Art is the truth and the straightest road to God." Karnofsky spewed out her philosophy as casually as if it were a laundry list.

"Have you seen…God"

"No."

"I want to see God."

"Well, knowing the existence of God, does not bring God. You must go to her. This requires will."

"How much is the fare…to Natchez?"

"I came into this world with everything. I was a princess. I lived in the court, the court on the Tura River. Ten dollars, you pose for me."

"When, now?"

"Now, the light is good now. Painting is color, and color is possible only with light. This light brings knowledge, which is virtue itself."

"There is light when I sing."

"You play in the clubs, and you see light?"

"I feel it."

"What do you see when you sing in these Jass Clubs?"

"Well, if I look out from the stage, I see shadows, the shadows of the dancers."

"Shadows, oh, yes." Karnofsky spoke matter of factly as she mixed her paints. "There is light in a cave. If you see shadows, though, turn around to look at the light. The shadows are ignorance, a wound on the intellect. There is no God in the shadows. If there is no God, any evil is possible from the wicked seeds of Adam."

"No, the shadows are good, they are just people resting at night." Honey Boy felt as though he were in a dream.

"Oh, you *are* a poet, this is fine. Poetry is stronger than philosophy. Poetry is real; philosophy is all theory. There is no love in philosophy. Come now, I paint you."

Honey Boy sat on a haystack facing the easel and holding his cornet across his lap.

"Play."

"Honey Boy raised his horn to his lips and began Strauss's "Blue Danube."

"No, no, no, play Jass. I left all that formality nonsense in St. Petersburg. Play your American Jass, play it hot."

Honey Boy proudly ripped into "Honey Boy's Blues."

"Yes, yes, yes." Karnofsky rejoiced.

Karnofsky did not bother to sketch before painting; so developed were her brush skills that she did not need a sketch as guide. Honey Boy played every song he could think of until the sun dropped and took the golden hues of the early evening with it.

Karnofsky brought in some loose hay, some kindling, and a few split logs, threw them in the middle of the barn, poured linseed oil on the pile, and lit the pile with a flint and knife. The blaze warmed the barn and filled it with a flickering orange-golden light, which burned well after midnight. The smoke mostly drafted out the bale loft door on the front wall of the barn; the rest hazed the air lightly and created undulations in the light between Karnofsky and Honey Boy. The reflections of the cornet changed constantly as Honey Boy played and Karnofsky painted.

The deep night sky of spring clouded over.

"Honey Boy Plays Midnight Serenade" would be Karnofsky's highest priced painting, fetching $1200 at first sale in New York and $1.8 million at auction in Beijing a century later.

As the fire light dimmed, Karnofsky turned the canvas to show Honey Boy his likeness. He felt more in a dream than before.

Some folks stay

Some folks go

Some folks come

Some folks know

"Why not go to Natchez, now, catch the Mississippi Queen, here's $20."

After a two hour nap, Honey Boy rose just before dawn began walking back to New Orléans to catch a boat to Natchez. He wondered all the way what Natchez and the millionaires looked like, and what his dad did there…and…why.

The Second Time

The second time Honey Boy saw his Beatricia she was milking a cow down by the river in the drying mud. Four years had passed. She was more beautiful than before. Her shirtwaist was light yellow this time covered by an ivory dairy apron. She had her hair pulled up high in a bonnet, so Honey Boy could see more of her neck. Her deep black skin was all the prettier against the yellow linen of her shirtwaist. Her feet were bare and a glowing pink on the soles, like a baby's feet that had never touched ground. Her handwork on the utters was efficient and gentle; she made it all seem as natural as morning dew. He stood awhile in awe, not fully trusting his eyes, and wanting to call out, but did not.

"Mornin' Mr.," she greeted looking up from her work.

"Yes, hello…Beatricia."

"It's 'Bee,' just 'Bee'." She reminded him.

"Bee, Bee, just Bee. Yes."

"You're up early for a music man, no?" Bee smiled warmly.

"No, I'm just going home…to see my, my father."

"I see." She stood slowly, gathering her milk pail, walked toward the tired music man and offered, "would you like the cream?" Her voice was kind and soft. She displayed both poise and humility in her walk, but the sincere gaze of her eyes, when he looked up from her neck, enchanted.

"Well?

"Yes, indeed, I would love some," Honey Boy replied, slowly and quietly breaking his reverie. He sipped the early morning cream from the tin milk pail of his beloved. It was warm and fresh and sweet. He returned the pail and wondered aloud, "how could I write a song…"

"Yes?" Bee asked after a long pause.

"A song…as sweet as this morning?"

"Well…I suppose I don't know, but if you ever do, I should want to hear it," she smiled as she trudged out of the sticky riverbank. "Bye, now."

New Orléans has ever been the lowest, muddiest, and flattest city in North America, most of it actually below sea level. This fact becomes readily apparent when the rains fall but do not drain—for days. It is something of a marvel that the city drains at all. Over 40 percent of the continental runoff (from as far away as New York and Montana) flows past New Orléans on its way to the Gulf of Mexico. And all that mud. Mud, mud, mud. A mud that never fully dries.

"Good bye?" He hung on each word as he watched his earthy, earthly angel walk away without looking back, the second time, at the one who started it all. "Wait, can I help you?"

Bee looked over her shoulder, "Sure, you want to carry one of these pails?"

"Oh, of course," Honey Boy hurried to catch up to her. "I could carry both," he offered.

"Okay, I'll carry your trumpet, then."

"Oh, that would be fine, but it's actually a cornet."

Bee traded the tin pails for the brass cornet in brown paper bag. "So what's the difference? Looks like a cornet to me." Bee drew the cornet from the bag and traced her eyes around its curves and valves and bell.

"Well, it just a little bit smaller, but it actually sounds different, too. Anyway, I like the tone better."

"Is it louder?"

"No, no it's just sweeter."

"Sweeter?"

"Well, it's mellower." Honey Boy checked Bee's reaction, hoping she understood. He didn't know how else to explain it, and he didn't want to seem arrogant to her.

"Mellower, that sounds nice."

Honey Boy inhaled slowly. Exhaled. "Yes, yes, it is nice. Do you…do you play music?"

"No," Bee shook her head slightly, "I sing, though."

"Oh, that sounds nice. What do you sing?"

"Gospel," Bee hesitated, "and blues."

"Blues?" Honey boy revealed his excitement in his voice.

"Well, sure. Nothing wrong with singing away your troubles."

"No, no, nothing wrong with that. I love the blues. I've been playin' the blues for years."

"Really, what songs do you know?"

"Oh, I know lots."

"Which ones, though; let's sing one."

Honey Boy's mind went blank. "Okay, go ahead, I'll sing along."

Bee thought for a second, "How about 'Down By the Riverside'?"

I stand here a waitin'

Down by the riverside

Honey Boy responded,

Yes, I left my love a waitin'

Down by the riverside

They sang together,

We'll be back together some day

Some day, some day

Gonna see my love some day

Honey Boy began the second verse,

Goin' off to make some money

Up in Chi ca go

Bee responded,

He's gonna buy me clothes and candy

Up in that big, big city

They sang together,

We'll be back together one day

One day, one day

Our day's a comin' soon.

Honey Boy's voice faltered on the last note. Bee laughed.

Honey Boy apologized in embarrassment, "Oh, sorry." Bee laughed harder. Honey Boy blushed and joined the laughter as they approached Bee's house.

"Shhhh, my grandma's probably sleeping."

"Oh, sorry, sorry. My grandma gets up earlier than everyone else in my house."

"Yeah, mine used to…then she got ill." Bee's mood turned sad.

"Oh, is she…" Honey Boy didn't know what to say.

Honey Boy walked quietly up to the back porch, set the milk pails down gently and turned to Bee for his cornet.

"Thanks, next time I'll invite you in."

"Sure." Honey Boy turned to leave. Bee blew him a kiss and smiled softly.

Honey Boy stood speechless and motionless, thinking of how different Bee was from all the painted girls of Storyville.

No need to worry

Don't ask why

Just wink and smile

Light the sky

Storyville boasted the first electrically illuminated saloon in American history when Tom Anderson opened his business equipped with 100 ceiling bulbs and electric sign in front his establishment. Five years later, in 1906, the District hosted the grand French Ball complete with contest to crown a "Queen." The price of admission had risen to three dollars, from two dollars the year prior. To keep an eye on the girls, Miss Jean Gordon formed the Society for the Prevention to Cruelty to Children to ensure that no minors appeared in the brothels.

Bee turned, took milk the pails, and silently entered the back door.

Honey Boy watched her as she disappeared into the cedar plank shotgun shack. A light glowed from the hearth and through the back window.

Home.

Beatricia.

Honey Boy.

Smoke rose from the chimney, but no sounds emerged from Bee's home.

Honey Boy walked backwards, slowly.

Watching.

Hoping.

Wanting.

Finally turning away and back up to the road. The road to the docks. The docks where he would take the riverboat to Natchez…and Father.

He looked over his shoulder once before Bee's house was out of sight.

She was standing on the back porch.

Honey Boy stopped to look.

She raised her index finger slowly to cross her lips vertically. "Shhhhhh," she mimed.

Honey Boy had no idea what she wanted him to do.

She glanced up at an overturned rowboat up the bank an motioned that way by nodding her head and pointing her eyes.

Honey Boy pointed toward the rowboat.

Bee smiled and walked that way.

Honey Boy joined her.

Bee skipped the last dozen feet.

Honey Boy could not help but smile at her playfulness.

"Well, can you row, Honey Boy?"

"I don't—"

"That's okay, land lover, I can. Just help me get her in."

The skiff was unnamed but in fine condition. Its lap-strake planks sported fresh varnish over a black keel, white hull, and claret top trim. The oars were clear spruce but also freshly varnished. Its four foot width and twelve foot length was perfect size for two.

Honey Boy grabbed the stern, Bee the bow as they righted the craft and set it in the river alcove gently, rippling the morning water. Bee graciously offered Honey Boy to board first; she made a grand sweeping circular motion with her right hand as she held the boat steady with her left. Honey Boy stepped first one foot, steadied himself, then the other, and sat down quickly as the boat rocked side to side.

Side to side.

Side to side.

Not stopping.

Honey Boy looked up at Bee; she was smiling. "Are you okay? I just wanted you to know what it felt like to hit a wake. If a steamboat comes by that's what it will feel like."

Bee boarded the stern effortlessly, took up one oar, and paddled on alternating sides facing forward as if in a canoe. "Okay, were clear, we have to switch places, so I can row stronger." Bee noticed a look of concern covering Honey Boy's face. "Okay, just sit there, and I'll go first."

Bee stood tall, took three poised steps to sit in front of Honey Boy as he held his plank seat tightly. Bee kept her eyes on the horizon, balancing the boat skillfully. She faced the stern, planted her feet squarely and used the strength of her legs in concert with her arm motion to row the boat with power.

"Okay, we're gliding now. You can cross over me and get to the back of the boat." Honey Boy crouched and slid his hand down the side of the skiff as he moved from the front seat plank, stepping over the middle plank where Bee sat, to the back seat plank. He sat quickly, relieved to be dry.

"What are you doing?"

Honey Boy looked over his shoulder at Bee. "What?"

"Why are you facing the back of the boat?" Bee grinned.

Honey Boy turned from his waist to face Bee, "I dunno, I just…I thought…you're facing that way…"

"Who's gonna steer?"

Honey Boy picked up his feet, raised them over the seat plank, and faced Bee, "Okay…how's this?"

"Fine, tell me where to go." Bee awaited directions.

Honey Boy scanned the riverscape, saw an overhanging willow on the other bank. He pointed, "how about there?"

Bee looked across the calm flowing waters. "Well, that's almost a mile—across current."

"Oh, is that too far?" Honey Boy looked up at a barge floating downriver, then down into the murky water.

Bee looked across the river, then back at Honey Boy, "I can get us there, for sure, but I'll need to rest a while before we row all the way back. I'm still tired from my morning chores. I've been up since five."

"Well…"

Bee began to row with long, smooth, strong strokes; each one just like the last a rhythm of plops, swooshes, whirls, and drips.

Plop.

Swoosh.

Whirl.

Drip.

Plop.

Swoosh.

Whirl.

Drip.

Plop.

Swoosh.

Whirl. Bee let the oars rest in their holders, tilting the paddles up in the air and resting the handles on the bottom of the boat. She scooted back and sat between the middle and front seat plank as she crossed her feet and rested her head on the side of the boat. "Are you scared?"

"Of what?"

"Anything."

"I don't think about it."

"Think about what?"

"Being scared."

Bee sat up to look at Honey Boy in the eyes. "What if—"

"I don't have time for 'what if'," Honey Boy adjusted his collar and looked down at his feet. "There's water in the boat, you know."

"It's just the river. The boat belongs to the river. It's only fair; if the river carries the boat, then the boat should carry the river."

"We're not going to sin—"

"Can't you swim?"

"Sure, but what about my horn?"

"Well, I guess you better play something on it, then, while you still have a chance, Mr. Honey Boy," Bee flirted.

Honey Boy loosened his collar. "I don't…what…I'm not…but…I, I, I—"

"Play me something sweet. Make me fall in love with you. I dare you."

Sweat began to bead on Honey Boy's temple as the two drifted silently down the middle of the river.

Silence.

Drifting.

Silence.

"What if I can't?"

"Is that what you're scared of?"

Silence.

"I don't know."

"Yes you do…you want to be the greatest ever, don't you?"

"What if I can't?"

"What if you can!"

"Maybe I'm not as good as everyone says."

"Maybe you are!" Bee sat up and started rowing again. "Do you think I can row us all the way there and all the way back?"

"Yeah, sure…I don't know."

"Then why did you take a chance on me?" Bee rowed swifter.

Silence.

"Why did you take a chance…" Honey Boy stopped mid-sentence.

"Just play me a song, Honey Boy. The sweetest song…ever," Bee yelled up into the sky.

"What if I can't?" Honey Boy raised his voice unintentionally.

"What if I can't," Bee looked over her shoulder at the barge drifting downriver, "beat that barge?" Be rowed still swifter.

Honey Boy looked up at the looming barge drifting on something of a collision course with their current route. "Why don't you…just—"

"Why don't you just take a chance." Bee rowed still swifter. "Or…do you want me to stop?"

Silence.

Bee rowed still swifter, panting, straining, sweating.

THWACK.

SWOOOOSHH.

Whirl.

"Heeeehaaaw!" Bee celebrated passing just in front of the barge, glancing it with her upriver oar to protect the skiff from damage.

They drifted, whirling slowly in the wake as the barge drifted away and the skiff settled back into the river.

Silence.

Honey Boy held back the vomit pushing up against his tonsils.

Bee leaned forward, took her mother's handkerchief from her skirt pocket, and wiped Honey Boy's brow. "Close your eyes."

Honey Boy closed his eyes and exhaled in relief. Bee kissed his closed eyelids—each three times. She took his hand in hers, "play me a song…the most beautiful song…a brand new song…a song just for me…and you." Honey Boy opened his eyes.

"No, play it with your eyes closed."

"I can't…I feel funny with my eyes closed." Honey Boy wanted back on dry land.

"I feel tired, too tired to row us home. Play for me, Honey Boy. Inspire me."

"Let's just go back," Honey Boy look toward Bee's house.

"No, we have to make the Willows on the other side before we can go back." Bee reminded Honey Boy of their challenge.

"Alright," Honey Boy reluctantly agreed and began playing "Honey Boy's Blues."

"No, not a blues," Bee protested, "I said the prettiest song ever. Just look over at those willows on the bank and play whatever comes to your mind."

Honey Boy looked over at the grass in the shade below the willows on the bank where they headed. He began to play.

"Yes," Bee began to row again, "that's pretty."

Honey Boy changed to a minor key.

"No, don't make it said, keep it pretty," Bee insisted.

Honey Boy changed back to 'C' major.

Bee rowed and rowed. Honey Boy improvised verse after verse, each becoming lighter as they approached the willows. Bee pulled mightily on the oars one final stroke to coast into the muddy bank just beneath the willows. Bee reached up for a handful of dangling branches to lift herself up onto shore with one hand as she held the skiff with the other. "Come on," she urged Honey Boy. He mimicked by grabbing branches in both hands and climbed ashore with relief. Bee sat in the grass and smoothed her skirt. "Lay your head in my lap, Honey Boy."

Honey Boy relaxed in relief as he set his cheek on Bee's lap. He could feel the warmth of her muscular thighs through her skirt. He quickly fell asleep. Bee watched him, then fell asleep herself as the willow branches swayed in the spring breeze and the Mississippi passed by. The skiff, stuck in the mud, rocked slightly in the river's undulations. The sun sparkled on the gentle ripples.

Mississippi Queen

A. Man Rey read the light off the water to gauge its depth. He once read in a riverboat captain's manual that "Darker water indicates deeper water."

"Three port." Rey called to the young, white lieutenant.

"Aye," replied the black engine's mate.

Over the years Rey had developed his own method for judging the depth of the water based on color, which indicated sand, mud, rock or grass. The hue of each told Rey how far below the surface the bottom lay.

"Six starboard."

"Aye."

Rey loved the River and working on it, especially the fringe benefit of claiming any items passengers left behind. Rey long ago ceased collecting coats, umbrellas, or hats, instead concentrating on newspapers, magazines, and books: *The Times Picayune, Beyond Good and Evil, The Complete Works of William Shakespeare, Uncle Tom's Cabin, The Cleveland Plain Dealer, Life on the Mississippi, Paradise Lost, The Raven and Other Poems of Edgar Allan Poe, Pride and Prejudice, The Federalist Papers, Narrative of the Life of Frederick Douglass*, and his favorite, *The Atlantic Monthly*. Rey was the best read man in town, black or white, and *the* guide of distinction and choice

amongst riverboat captains on the Natchez stretch of the
Mississippi River.

"Engines half."

"Engines half," Captain Charles Lee Black confirmed.

Rey was not a riverboat captain, for that was hardly allowed.
Although there was United States Congressman Robert Smalls
from South Carolina who, as slave, had commandeered the
Confederate Navy transport ship, *The Planter*, and delivered to the
Union, Mississippi riverboat captains were still almost exclusively
white in Rey's time. Rey was an unofficial pilot; he told the
captain where to steer—and where not to steer.

Lieutenant Holbrook approached the Captain, "Is it proper for
us to take orders from a black man, Captain?

"A. Man Rey knows every sandbar, shoal, mudbar, and stump
10 miles either side of Natchez, Lieutenant."

"Do we know his credentials, sir?"

"He has a perfect record."

"Perfection, how can a negro be perfect?" the lieutenant
objected.

"No groundings in 11 years of service—seems perfect to me."

Certain people belong in certain places. Rey didn't belong in
New Orléans; Rey belonged in Natchez.

Natchez was a creation of commerce. It lay 199 nautical miles
up the river from New Orléans—and a world apart. Though it was
the site of alternate slaughters of French by natives and, then,
natives by French in the eighteenth century, Natchez escaped the
Civil War unscathed. After the war, Natchez boomed with not just

cotton but logging and goods coming down from Ohio or up from the Gulf of Mexico. Natchez wold later take homage from Native son Richard Wright in "The Voodoo of Hell's Half-Acre" and no fewer than nine steamboats plying the mighty river above and below its harbor with the town's name emblazoned on stern and bow. There were no famous madams, no infamous brothels, and no mile-long parades, but there were plenty of millionaires—more than in New Orléans or any other American city at the turn of the twentieth century.

As always, Rey guided the *Mississippi Queen* masterfully through an obstacle course of submerged hazards for ten miles to the Natchez harbor. As Honey boy and the other passengers alighted from the gangplank to the dock, Rey tied-off the ship at stern and bow.

Honey Boy and Rey caught eyes. Rey had heard rumors that his estranged son was on his way and recognized himself in Honey Boy's face. Honey Boy recognized himself in Rey, especially his eyes. It took his breath.

"Golden, Mr. Golden?" Honey Boy called, stepping on shore.

"Rey, I go by Rey now." He called back from the dock as he finished tying-off the boat.

"Rey?"

"A. Man Rey...the Nubian God of Sun."

"Yes, yes, I know." Honey Boy was proud to show his education to his father.

"Where you stayin' in town, boy?" Rey paused his work and looked up to gaze Honey Boy eye-to-eye.

"I got work here at the Rhythm Club."

"Work? You're gonna work at the Rhythm Club?"

"Yes, sir." Honey Boy raised his cornet in its brown paper bag case.

"Where are you staying?"

Honey Boy quietly replied, "The Club, they have a room for traveling musicians."

Rey paused. "Why don't you come back to the homestead?

"Well—"

"Let me talk to you awhile, son." Father joined son on shore. The two walked silently at first down the shore and headed upriver a half-mile, then stopped on the bank by a willow tree overhanging the bank a quarter-mile from the homestead. "I heard you were coming...so what are your plans, Honey Boy?"

"How did you know my name?"

Rey paused before responding. "How's your mother?"

"She needs her violin."

"What about you? Why did you come all the way up here?"

"I'm gonna live here a while." Honey Boy held his breath.

Rey paused before responding. "With your $2 second-hand coronet you probably bought on the corner of Rampart and Perdido from some gambler, pimp, prostitutes, thief, beggar, or politician?

"No, mother never lets me consort with politicians."

"But why here? This is a town for millionaires—"

"So, what about you?" Honey Boy was becoming light-headed.

"I'm a riverboat man. Someday I'll be a *bona fide* pilot. If I live long enough, I'll be a captain."

"Why here, though?"

"This is where I make my mark. This is where my reputation is." Rey looked out on the water, up the river to his right, then down the river to his left, slowly.

"Why can't I make my mark here?"

"Cotton is still king here; the Mississippi is Queen, and Natchez is the Queen's jewel, but this is not a music town. It's a business town. N'orlunz is a music town."

Honey Boy looked over his shoulder back toward town. "What if I make Natchez a music town?"

Rey looked at Honey Boy to gauge his resolve. Rey smiled slightly, "How long do you think that would take?"

Honey Boy looked back at Father as he measured his response. "I don't know, a week."

"A week?" Father stroked his chin, shook his head, and chuckled. "Alright, you can stay here two weeks while you re-invent Natchez, but no noise at night when you get home; Sadie and the baby need their sleep."

"Why don't I just stay down in the boathouse on the river? Then I won't bother anyone."

"Rats."

"Rats?"

Father Golden pointed to the floating foundation of the boathouse as a rat waddled across a pontoon. "One bite won't kill you as fast as a water moccasin, but you'll be just as dead in a fortnight."

"From a rat?"

"From Black Plague; killed half of Europe. Killed Ian Anderson, that's how I got my first job—a white man died, and I was at the right place at the right time." Father and son sat quietly on the bank as the sun set and the cicadas sang their evening serenade. The grass was wet from an afternoon rain and still smelled sweet. Honey Boy mimicked Father and pulled a tall blade from its root, snapped it in half, and sucked on the broken end. It tasted like country, like nothing he had ever tasted in New Orléans. Green, ripe, and raw. The rough but tiny ridges on the shaft caught on Honey Boy's tongue as he tried to pull the blade out of his mouth, so he swallowed it instead and wondered how the horses and cows sustained themselves on such meager fare.

Father just stared at the river passing by. The river was alive, it was time, it was life, it was everything. Honey Boy leaned back until fully supine, making a bed of the green grass. He stared up at the darkening sky. The light just after sunset was Honey Boy's favorite color. It was the color of his music, deep blue—a blue as deep as the universe, past all the stars and planets, a blue that emanated from the beginning of time and would glimmer until the end.

Dusk.

"Let's get on back to the house, son," Father interrupted Honey Boy's reverie.

"Yessir, I'm playin' the second and third set at the Rhythm Club tonight." Father and son walked uphill toward the homestead.

"You got a girl in N'Orlunz?"

"Yes…no…not yet, but her name's Beatricia. I wrote her a song."

"Did she like it?"

"She will."

"You wrote your girl a song, and you haven't played it for her yet?" Father and son both laughed.

"I could marry me one of these old rich men, Nora." Bessie had never been to Natchez before, but she liked the thought of being around millionaires.

"Never happen," Nora advised knowingly; she had grown up just outside of town, down on the river in a shantytown that disappeared every several years or so, whenever the river rose more than seven feet. Nora suffered no illusions of marrying a millionaire. They were all white. She was not. Nora was not even an octaroon or quadroon. Nora was not even a mulatta; she was an anti-octaroon—not one-eighth black, but one-eighth white. These distinctions mattered. She could not even hope for an unofficial mistress status, so she didn't. She was black, proud of it, and was perfectly content to marry a black man.

"The sun is down, can we go downstairs now?" asked Bessie.

"No, wait until some more dancers show up, then we can mingle in unnoticed." Nora's uncle ran the Rhythm Club and had agreed to let Nora and Bessie stay "just one night" in the loft where travelling musicians slept on their way through town. Since there was a local band playing, the loft was free, but only until Friday when Big Black Bill arrived with his piano accordion, twelve-string guitar, and a thousand-and-one stories, each one funnier than the last.

"How we gonna get this bottle to Honey Boy, Bessie? Little David's not gonna give us the other $20 unless we do his deed."

"Don't you worry, Mr. Honey Boy's a man. I know how to handle any man with two eyes." Bessie grinned and raised her eyebrow.

"We don't even know where he is."

"But he's coming here tonight. David got him the gig."

"So why would he talk to us?" Nora grew impatient.

"Easy, we'll go talk to him during break, tell him how much we like his music, and how we heard him down river, and we're so pleased to find him here at your uncle's place. Then, at midnight, we bring him David's bottle as a gift, and *voila*."

"What's in that bottle, anyway?" Nora was growing more suspicious than curious.

"I don't know, some special whiskey. Supposed to make Honey Boy change his sound, make him sound fancier so David can get him some fancier gigs." Bessie was not curious. This was just business.

"Why didn't David just give him the bottle himself?"

"I don't know, maybe David tried but Honey Boy was too proud."

"Since when is a drinker too proud to take whiskey from another drinker?" Nora was annoyed now.

"Who cares? Let's just do David's deed and get on with our own business. Jasmine wants us back tomorrow for the Friday night crowd."

The Rhythm Club was eleven feet above flood level and just outside Natchez proper. It was a dance hall and bar a bit too grand to be called a juke joint. Although it was in the black section of town, plenty of white folk wandered in, especially when a band with a reputation played.

From the outside The Rhythm Club resembled more a barn than anything else with its unpainted cedar vertical plank siding and shingle roof. The windows all originally had glass in them, but most had been broken—from the inside—over the years. The bar itself was a single felled cypress plank eighteen-feet long and plenty worn by bottles, elbows, and glasses. The place smelled of corn liquor, which sold by the shot, the glass, or the jug, depending on how temporarily rich and reckless the customer was. Once the sun went down three gas lights dimly glowed just brightly enough so that patrons could make out the band, the bar, the bathrooms, and the front and back doors. The stage was a mere eighteen inches high and the musician's loft hung over it at eight feet, leaving just six-and-a-half feet head room, which was barely enough for Big Black Bill. The floor was always dusty or muddy, according to season, and it masked whatever wood lay underneath it. There were two dozen tables covering the floor nearest the front door, the bar and stools on the river side, the stage opposite the front door, which left just enough dance floor for about twenty couples to dance to a fast number or forty for a slow song.

Sometimes sixty squeezed in on Saturday nights. It was twice as big, but not even half as infamous, as the Funky Butt Jass Club down in New Orléans.

The cops rarely bothered to raid the place, mostly because both the patrons and the owner were too poor to pay any bribes, and the jail was barely big enough to hold a dozen real criminals. That left no room for four dozen relatively innocent revelers. Then too, there was nothing illegal going on, so a raid would not serve justice or any moral purpose. And besides, the Sunday choir's unofficial practice was before the first set on Saturday night, and no decent citizen would want to interfere with that.

Honey Boy punched and bounced through his scales nine times while walking from his father's homestead to The Rhythm Club. He wore his best white linen shirt, burgundy wool knit tie, and a blue gabardine suit his father lent him. It was double-breasted and fit well, but was a bit warm for the season. Honey Boy sported it famously, though, and it accentuated his broad shoulders and military posture. He wore some walking shoes to town to avoid dusting up his just-shined black oxfords. Father watched his son march away as if watching a one man parade of joyous splendor. Father filled with a mix of pride for what Honey Boy had become and resentment for not having guided his son to manhood. There was only a fortnight left until Honey Boy Golden would turn eighteen and legally become a man.

What could a father do in two short weeks?

"Father?" called Sadie after her husband.

Rey put down the book he was reading "I'm out on the porch."

"Come sing your baby girl back to sleep. You know she likes your lullabies more than mine." Father more hummed than sang his lullabies, but they were just as soothing all the same. The only intelligible lyrics he sang were "mommy," "daddy," "baby," and "Billie," the girl child's Christian name.

Baby Billie was asleep in minutes. Mother and Father settled into their rocking chairs on the porch.

"Did you ask Honey—"

"Yes," Father interrupted, "He knows to be quiet when he comes home."

"He isn't going to toot his horn all the way back from town is he?"

"No. He's a musician, not a moron."

"Pssst. Look who just walked in." Bessie nudged Nora.

"Let's do our deed, then, and get to bed; I want to rest up for the trip home."

"Miss Nora, how are you gonna sleep through all this racket when your bed is right over the top of the bandstand?"

Nora sighed.

"Just make the best of it and have your fun, Miss Nora. You'll be back at work tomorrow. We have rehearsal at Fisk in the afternoon before we go to Jasmine's."

"What, I thought David was going to stand in for us? Nora became more agitated as the night wore on. How can we even get back in time? The Riverboat is gonna take all day. We may not even be back to open Jasmine's." Nora could not afford to lose her high-paying job.

"Keep an eye on Honey Boy," Bessie ordered.

"He's playin' the second set."

"How do you know?"

"My uncle told me." Nora looked at the clock behind the bar.

Midnight.

Honey Boy steps onstage, sits on a pine milk crate turned on its side and placed just in front of the drummer. He calls out, "Medium shuffle rag in B-flat. Let's make the angels weep and the Devil sigh, boys"; he taps the tempo on the stage floor with the bell of his coronet.

"Let 'em have it," calls out "Haystack," the trombonist, as he cocks his black bowler back on his giant head and follows Honey Boy's impromptu lead. The dancers, who usually step right in on such a juicy number, just stand and listen in delight and awe at the clarity of Honey Boy's infectious melody and the genius of his original musicality.

Bup-Baaaah Bah

Bup-Baaaah Bah

Bup Bup Bup Bup Bup Bup Bup Bup Bup-Baaaah Bah…

The second 32-bar chorus is a variation on the first, so the crowd surges onto the floor rejoicing in the most joyous tunes ever played, heard, or felt in Natchez. The dancers swing wilder and freer than ever. The power and drive are as rough as pig iron, but the tone of "the one who started it all" is pure honey. A single bead of sweat forms on Honey Boy's forehead just next to the vein that always bulged when he played it hot.

Swing.

Honey Boy stands up to swing a second song, smiles at the crowd and announces, "We're gonna pick it up a pace with this number I've been workin' on; let's just call it 'The Rhythm Club Jump'." The crowd roars, and not a soul remains seated. Honey Boy looks out over the dancers, holds his coronet at his side, and croons:

Flesh and bone

Trumpet and trombone

No need to dance alone

At the Rhythm Club

We're gonna

Jump

Gut-bucket guitar

Ole Cypress bar

Everyone's a star

At the Rhythm Club

Yeah

Jump

Honey Boy wipes his brow with his white handkerchief, licks his lips, raises his coronet to his mouth, and blows a variation on the melody.

Bwa Bwah Bwa

Bup-bah-bup-bah-bup-bah

Bah-bup-bup-bup-bah

Bup-bup-bup-bup-baaaaaaah

The dancers stop to cheer, Honey Boy bows his head slightly, smiles sincerely, and returns to his croon.

As a rule

Everyone's so cool

No need for charm school

At the Rhythm Club

O'er here

Jump

We got a man at the door

Hard wood floor

And dancin' galore

At the Rhythm Club

Whoa

Jump

If you ain't never been here
You better get here

I said

If you ain't never been here
You ain't been nowhere

Say again

If you ain't down here
Best Get on down here

Rhythm Club.

Jump.

Honey Boy doesn't wait for the applause to end before he begins a new tune. He leans back as his coronet shouts past his pewter wah-wah mute, and the dancers jump. "Haystack" growls on trombone as the dancers bounce. "Sticks," the sinewy Haitian drummer, thumps on his 28-inch bass kick drum as the dancers rattle the floor; then he taps on his cowbell just to amuse. "Goat," the silver-templed clarinetist, whines as the dancers bounce to the primal cries that pierce down through their bones and into their souls. *"C'est on arivee Monsieur L'Honey Boyee!"* shouts out a French-speaking Creole dancer who walked eleven miles down from the hills just to dance one night to the music of the prodigy from New Orléans. The band and the dancers become one, swept up in a frenzy of sweet and hot syncopation.

Bounce.

The night rolls on; Bessie and Nora have forgotten their mission. The dim gas light glows and reflects a warm and sultry hue on the faces of the dancers and musicians. The drive and excitement inspire. The band plays on. The crowd strikes its stride and raves on unpretentious, leaving all earthly worries far behind. Honey Boy shares his gift from God and nearly blows Gabriel from Heaven. The young dancers press on, wasting not a moment of their precious youth here; there is no love in vain, no fearing the light of day or the dark of night, no imitating Europe or Africa. This is America, a new America. The eagle is rockin' it— all night long.

Rave.

Crashing the party, the bartender steps onstage to announce, "Thank you for coming."

"One more song! One more song! One more song!" chant the dancers.

"Come back tomorrow night for Big Black Bill."

"Boooh!" a yell bellows from the corner.

"Honey Boy! Honey Boy! Honey Boy!" demand the dancers. Nora takes the opportunity to rush up to the stage and hand Honey Boy the bottle. "This is from Little David."

"Thank you…and David." Honey Boy sets the bottle on the stage floor next to the bass drum.

"You weren't supposed to tell him who sent it," Bessie whispers in Nora's ear as the two turn and walk back into the crowd.

Honey Boy relents: "Thank you all for coming, this will be our final number: 'Farewell Blues'." Honey Boy plays a full twelve-bar chorus intro while the rest of the band just listens to his coronet moan a melody more melancholy than any lyrics could ever convey, yet the power and light of his horn suffuse a promise into his blues that transcend any sadness. The band lilts in on the second chorus, hanging on every beat. The couples embrace, leaning into each other, swaying in unison and slowly moving across the floor.

Sway.

Dawn pours rudely through the windows. The dancers part with a standing ovation for the one who started it all. The three middle-class white couples in the crowd join in unmolested and almost unnoticed. The pianos in their parlors at home have plenty of sheet music upon them and many a lesson taught at them, but nothing has ever come out of them that sounds like this. This is new. This is spontaneous and raw, but there is nothing crude about it. This is genius—pure American genius.

Tonight is at once a funeral for the old ways and a parade for this new sound that just donned the name "jass," maybe after the jasmine perfume preferred by the prostitutes in the brothels that bore the music, maybe after a Jamaican slang term for sex, or maybe after a slurred contraction for "music driving so hard that it's kickin' ya in *j'ass!*"

Whatever the origin of its name, and however the spelling soon switched its two final letters, Jazz was as uniquely American as Old Glory herself, following, leading, and wandering into the future. This jazz was sometimes uneducated, always unpredictable, but never unsophisticated.

Don't waste time

Seize the day

Like a farmboy

Makin' hay

The Astors and Vanderbilts may have been the toast of New York, but Honey Boy Golden was the jass legend of New Orléans and now owned the key to the city of Natchez. John Philip Sousa and Enrico Caruso were already selling music recordings for the Victrola company, but it wasn't long before Irving Berlin and a host of others would try to cash in on the Jazz craze. Friends began to urge Honey Boy to play with a handkerchief over his hand so no one could steal his fingering.

"My music doesn't come from my fingers," is all he would ever say in reply.

Honey Boy sang and smiled all the way back to his father's homestead.

"Good morning,' little darlin'," he called to his sister, who was crawling around the front porch. She cooed and rolled over on her back watching Honey Boy walk up the path. Sadie smiled at her stepson. She was a handsome bride only two years Honey Boy's senior. Sadie boasted many talents, mostly domestic. "Catfish and eggs for breakfast…hungry?"

"Yes ma'am, and thirsty." Honey Boy had been hoping for breakfast all the way home.

"You'll have to go out to the barn if you want milk, otherwise I have some sweet tea leftover from yesterday."

"Yes ma'am, tea would be fine." Honey Boy sat down at the table and noticed a banjo in the corner. "You play?"

"Sometimes."

"I bet you play like a party."

"Probably not as good as you're accustomed to."

After breakfast Honey Boy handed Sadie the banjo and picked up two spoons to play a rhythm. Sadie hesitated, then walked out onto the porch where Baby and Father were rocking in a chair in the early morning sun. Sadie strummed quietly at first, then fuller. She sang softly, "*Home, sweet home…*" She hummed the next verse. Baby Billie rolled over, buried her face in Father's chest, and began to nod off. Honey Boy brushed the spoons softly up and down his sleeve. Sadie's hum was motherly and soothing. A warmth glowed from Sadie and blanketed the entire home.

Baby and Father fell asleep.

Honey Boy curled up in the grass beneath the cottonwood trees to sleep.

Sadie gazed out over the river, still humming her tune. Then she joined the rest in a nap.

Dream.

"Honey Boy, come inside for dinner."

"I will, Father, I just gotta clean up first." Honey Boy walked to the well, pumped a few handfuls of water, washed his face, straightened his clothes, and went inside for supper.

Sadie offered Honey Boy a stool at the table. "Will you be playing tonight?"

"Yes ma'am; you should come by and sing with us."

"I'm sure I'm very flattered, but I don't have a proper dress, and I have the baby." Sadie looked over at her husband. Father looked at Honey Boy sternly.

"Right, well, we can play some more tomorrow, then." Honey Boy smiled sincerely.

"Have you remade Natchez yet, son?"

"I'm workin' on it. Tonight I'm gonna hit high 'G' at least once."

"High 'C'?" Sadie had never heard of anyone going so high on a coronet.

"No ma'am, high 'G,' it's above 'C' a few notes."

"On that coronet?" Sadie was intrigued.

"Yes ma'am."

Rey chuckled, "Son, you're gonna hit high 'G' with that $2 second-hand coronet you brought up here in a brown paper bag?"

The three laughed.

Baby Billie smiled and giggled.

"So, I was in Hell last night—no that was Memphis?" Big Black Bill waited for an uncomfortable laugh from the crowd to begin his set. Honey Boy smiled before joining in on the second verse.

Big Black Bill introduced each new song with a story or a one-liner: "Why did the preacher lay down his bible?...This next song is as sweet as your girl saying, 'yes'...Who was that woman I saw your husband with last night?...Grease up the griddle, we got a hot one for your fiddle...Abraham Lincoln, Frederick Douglass, and Robert E. Lee walk into a bar...Shimmy and shiver, this next song's goin' make you quiver...I'd go to Hell, or back to Memphis, to be able to play like this Honey Boy—from now on, you all can just watch his dust..."

Another all-night sensation and standing ovation—for Honey Boy. He bowed sincerely, shook hands with the dancers, and wiped his brow with his mother's handkerchief before packing his horn into its brown paper bag.

The bar ran out of liquor, but the crowd left slowly. Honey Boy made it home before dawn.

Big Black Bill wooed a tiny dancer he had been watching all night long. "I'm a very rich man, you know."

"Really? You have a big mansion here in town, Mr. Bill?"

"Certainly. Allow me to represent." Big Black Bill wandered down to the riverside with his female companion, gently holding her hand in one of his oversized palms; in the other he toted Honey Boy's gift from Little David. Big Black Bill took swigs between sweet-little-nothings, pinches, and giggles all the way to the boathouse. "Come on over here, little honey."

"Up in there? What's in there?"

"It's a boat in a house. It's a houseboat."

"This is your mansion?"

"It's a friend of mine's. I stay here whenever I'm in town." Big Black Bill stepped into Rey's 18-foot skiff, all but sinking it with his 280 pounds. His date, Coco, gingerly came aboard with her 95-pounds. Big Black Bill nestled his square-jawed face into the crook of Coco's neck. He lay down, pulling her atop. The skiff rocked, splashing and taking on a few gallons of river.

"Careful, careful," worried Coco.

"Come here, babydoll." Big Black Bill encircled Coco with a giant bear hug, then suddenly opened his eyes as wide as the Mississippi.

"What, what's wrong?"

"Just sing me a sweet little song, get me goin'."

"What? You sloppy oaf, you brought me all the way down here, and you're too drunk to do anything about it!" Coco scowled.

"No, no, nothin' like that, babydoll, I always lay it down, sugar; I just need some inspiration."

Coco screeched, "Eeeeeeeeew! What the hell is that?"

"What?"

"It's either a white raccoon or the biggest damn rat I ever seen!" Coco pushed herself off Big Black Bill; she crawled out onto the dock and ran to shore, up the hill, and back toward town.

Big Black Bill sat up slowly, turned around, and stared the varmint in its red eyes. "You look like my first wife, only prettier." The rat retreated soon after Big Black Bill fell back into the skiff in stupor, then sleep, snoring loudly.

Honey Boy was growing more and more restless after each passing day in Natchez. He played each night, slept until noon, then visited with Sadie and Billie each afternoon until dinner with Father. After dinner, father and son would read to each other before Honey Boy went off to the Rhythm Club. "Shall I compare thee to a summer's day…We hold these truths to be self-evident…Late in the afternoon of a chilly February day…In order to form a more perfect union…It was the best of times, it was the worst of times…Herein lie buried many things which if read with patience may show the strange meaning of being black…"

Honey Boy interrupted the seminar on the thirteenth night. "You have Mother's golden maple violin?"

"You gettin' homesick already, son? You just got here."

"Do you have it? I want to hear her play it."

"I sold it when the baby came. Needed a cow and some chickens."

"A cow and chickens for a golden maple violin?" Honey Boy's voice faltered.

"I can't be a free man in this country without my own homestead. A family needs a cow and some chickens. We can't eat catfish and poke salet all day."

"But where's the violin?"

"Honey Boy, it's 1906; you don't need a golden maple violin and neither does your mother. Learn from our history but make your own future. Live our constitution and make the Declaration of Independence come true."

"How?"

"A black man in America is still a man, even here in Dixie; you must constantly assert your manhood, but you must be diplomatic about it."

"What…what does that mean?"

"You mustn't challenge others, but you must rise to the challenge they bring. Put aside your sorrows and your worries, leave behind your misfortunes. Be clever, but, even more so, be wise. Mostly, be bold."

"What do I do?"

"Certain people belong in certain places."

"Where do I belong?" Honey boy fought back his growing nausea.

"Leave Natchez. This town is for millionaires, you're a simple man. Go back down the river. Go back to Beatricia. Go back to your mother. Go back to N'Orlunz. Go back home. Go make your music, play for your dancers, march in your parade.

"Why?"

"You must be who you are. Be Honey Boy Golden. Go hit the highest 'G'; be the one who started it all."

Honey Boy felt more confusion than inspiration. "Why, why, why can't I stay here?" The two avoided eye contact. Sadie looked up from her sewing. Rey had no more answers to give. Honey Boy waited and slowly realized that he did not want to hear one.

Honey Boy packed his satchel slowly the next day. He didn't play The Rhythm Club on his last night in the hometown of his father. He and Father played cribbage instead at the homestead— no reading. Sadie had sewn a burlap bag padded with cotton to carry Honey Boy's coronet. Father and son walked slowly to the dock after breakfast. Honey Boy, hollow-hearted, didn't look back once onboard. Father watched the boat steam downriver until it rounded the bend and was completely out of sight. Father felt empty as he walked slowly up the riverbank toward his boathouse.

"Hey Big Man, time to get up, I gotta catch some fish for dinner."

"*A-Man-Rey*," Big Black Bill sang in his best operatic baritone. "I'll go with you. I know where all the catfish hide."

"Oh, no. Last time we tried that, almost killed us both."

"Never mind the *S.S. Cleopatra* here; let's just walk up by that willow there."

"I only have one pole."

"Don't need no pole." Big Black Bill strolled up the bank to the willow, lay down on his big belly slowly, inched to the edge of the water where the willow overhung the bank. He rolled up his sleeve well past the elbow, submerged his balled fist as deep as it would go, and remained still for minutes.

"Stop playing, you big clown."

"Be patient, be patient. Catfish are almost blind. They'll take my hand for a trout and try to swallow it whole."

Another few minutes passed.

"Bill, I don't have time for—"

"Whoaa there!" Big Black Bill yanked his fist out of the water with a big splash and an even bigger catfish, its mouth wrapped around his fist. He knocked its head on the trunk of the old willow three times before the mammoth fish finally succumbed. "I'll drink to that." Big Black Bill handed the half-full bottle to his old Civil War comrade.

"A bit early for whiskey."

"Oh, but it's smooth as a hog's belly." Big Black Bill curled up like a baby under the willow, rubbed his own belly, and sang a gospel song he was still composing: "My Love is Deep, Lord."

My love is deep, Lord

Oh, so deep

Deeper than the Oceans

'Neath the Heavens

Deeper than the valleys

Below the highest mountains

My love is deep, Lord

Oh, so deep

Don't need a mansion

In London town

Bill began to smile.

Just need my lover

Sweet Fanny Brown.

Rey laughed. "I think that last verse needs some work."

"Maybe so," Bill joined in laughter.

Rey shook his head, took a slow sip, and spit it out, "Tastes like saltpeter."

The Highest "G"

Honey Boy could tell he was almost back to New Orléans by the taste of sea salt in the air. All the way down the river he composed a song in his mind.

Da-duh…da-duh…da-duh..da…duht…

Ba-duh da duh dut dah dut dah duh duuuhh…

Doo-doo doo doo…doo doo doo dooohh…

Bwah-bwah bu-bup bup bup bup bup bup BWAAAAHHH!

Honey Boy debuted his new song as he marched down past the Funky Butt Jass Club on his way back home.

"Now that's a beautiful song, son." Red commented, smiling at Honey Boy's return.

"It's for Beatricia," proclaimed Honey Boy, seriously.

"That's a song for anyone who has ever loved, my boy. That's a song for all time."

It wasn't a ballad. It wasn't a love song at all. It wasn't even a blues.

"It's not supposed to be beautiful, it's a stomp."

"A stomp is a joyous thing, Honey Boy; it makes you want to dance with someone all night long…and it doesn't get any more beautiful than that."

"I put double 'G,' in it."

"Yes sir. I heard it…up above 'double C' and 'double D' and 'double E' and 'double F'; yes sir, you did—'double G' it was."

It was dusk at the Funky Butt Jass Club, and not a dancer on the floor to hear the Big Noise as Honey Boy's one man parade passed by outside. Honey Boy played the highest note played before or since on a brass cornet.

"Why don't you play that tonight inside?" Red smiled proudly at his friend and student.

"It's not ready."

"Sounds ready to me."

Honey Boy looked up into the darkening sky, into that favorite color of his, "I'm not ready."

"Well, that's the sign of a wise man, and you just turned eighteen. You wait until you are good and ready."

"I gotta hit 'double G' 100-days in a row before I play it for an audience, and Beatricia."

"Yes, yes. That'll put you just in time for the Independence Day Parade."

"I need to start my own outfit. I want to call it The Freedom Marchers Brass Band."

"Get me a young horse to ride and this old mule will join you," Red beamed.

Honey boy smiled at the thought of Red on a horse. "Do you know how to ride?"

"No, so you better find me a horse who knows how to give a ride!"

"Okay, Big Bill Black will be in town, so he can sing with us. He has a big enough voice for outdoors."

"Let's get two more horses and a cart for Professor Tony and his piano."

"Who can we get for trombone?" Honey Boy became more and more enthusiastic.

"Let me see if I can talk to Danny Smith."

"Doesn't he have his own outfit?"

"Big Belly Blues Band? They haven't played since Toots went up to Saint Louie last Christmas."

"Okay, what about a drummer. We'll want a big bass drum."

"We'll get a bass drum and a snare. We'll out class 'em all."

"But who?"

"Ginger and her little sister."

"Girls?"

"We're gonna out class 'em all, Honey Boy…we'll be the pride of The District."

"Do the Baker girls live in Storyville?"

"Sure do, their mom works down at Delilah's."

"Missus Baker is a—"

"Cook. She's a cook."

"But can they play…loud…and are they strong enough to march all through town?" Honey Boy was skeptical.

"They march for hours in the Fisk band. Hours and hours. You remember how it was."

Honey Boy gazed into the almost dark sky. His favorite color was becoming black. The stars shone through more prominently. "What about a saxophone and a banjo?"

"Big Bill Black can play banjo or accordion and sing at the same time. He could probably play both and sing at the same time if he gets a notion." Red joked.

"Okay, but we will need a saxophone."

"Robert Stewart."

"Robert Stewart, from New York City?" Honey Boy had heard him play once on a street corner for a gathering crowd.

"Yes sir, every time he plays he's tellin' a story."

"Well, I heard him play once, the people sure liked him, but he seems too sophisticated for us down here."

"What's wrong with that? You're sophisticated." Red smiled with a charming warmth.

"Oh, maybe a little, but not like that. He plays symphonies…from sheet music."

"Have you seen him down at Congo Square on Sundays? He's funkier than a bald-headed monkey." Red laughed at his homespun epithet. "Let's go see him. Decide for yourself."

Honey Boy walked to Congo Square the next Sunday. He had been practicing his "double G" every day, 9 times a day. When Honey Boy arrived at 8 a.m. he was the second one, just after Red. Red was playing Flamenco music on his guitar and stomping his feet as accent. Soon a woman arrived with her marimba, which she played as she approached Red. Red began to play more suavely, matching the marimba. Three barefoot girls appeared and set the music to movement. Uninhibited, as 8-year old girls are, they danced freely from toe to tips of fingers. They lowered down to the ground, rose up on their toes, spun round and round, swirled their hips, undulated their arms, and rocked their heads to the rhythm.

A conga player soon joined them, matching their beat, watching their movements and trying to complement their dance. He alternately rubbed his hand across the skin of his drum, tapped it with finger tips, pounded it with his fist, or slapped it with his palm. He created a multitude of musical ideas from his single drum, two hands, and artistic imagination.

A very old man lugged in a tuba, which he could barely carry at his advanced age, but played with passion once he sat down with it and rested for a brief moment. His low notes added a triumphant quality to the songs. He played with all the pride of his 9th Texas Regimental Band of the Mexican-American War decades earlier.

More dancers of all ages and sizes arrived and surrounded the musicians, inspiring them to play more and more joyfully. Honey Boy joined them first without his cornet and later heeding calls from all quarters to play along.

A Polish Jew entered the mix with her violin, which she played with all the abandon of a gypsy. Her long hair covered her wizened face, hiding her wistful expressions, and almost toothless grin. She was a Sunday morning regular, though no one knew her name, where she came from, or where she went after the music ended.

The Baker girls marched in, one pounding on her bass drum, the other on her snare. They sported their Fisk uniforms, bright smiles, perfect posture, and jade bracelets. At eleven and thirteen, they weren't the youngest musicians at the event, but they were the most energetic and indefatigable, marching circles around the crowd for hours and hours.

It had been years since Honey Boy played the square. He played late Saturday nights and early Sunday afternoons, so he usually did chores for Mother on Sunday mornings. Since he hadn't played this Saturday, he arose at 5 a.m. this morning to do his work before coming to the square. He was beginning to dread the thought of leaving to go across town and play his usual Sunday afternoon gig at the Longshoreman's Hall down on the river.

Just before noon Robert Stewart rode in on a camel. The tall circus animal knelt down so Stewart could slide off its hump and onto the ground. Stewart sat down on a bench, unfolded the music stand, set out a three-fold score, assembled his reed, and began to play "Beethoven's Fifth Symphony," which Stewart transposed in his mind to the key of "B-flat" so as to match the other musicians. Several bars in, Stewart changed the melody to "Tiger Rag."

The crowd applauded.

Steward stood up and played an embellished variation the melody.

The crowd cheered.

Stewart leaned back and played the melody with a trill on each note, making his saxophone sound like a whinnying horse.

The crowd roared.

Stewart kicked over his music stand and played the melody with honks and bleats accents throughout.

The crowd erupted.

Honey Boy set down his cornet and clapped his hands.

Stewart bowed then invited, "come blow your horn, Little Boy Wonder."

Honey Boy smiled, picked up his cornet and set to it:

Bup bah bup bah bup bah

Stewart answered:

Bwup bwah bwup bwah bwup bwah

Honey Boy slowed it down, hanging on the beat:

Buuup baaaah buuup baaah buuup baaaah

Stewart slowed it down still more:

Bwuuuuuup bwaaaaaaah bwuuuuuup bwaaaaaah bwuuuuuup bwaaaaaaah bwaaaaaaaaaaaaaaaaaaaaaaaaaaaaaaaaaaaaaaaaaaaaaaaaah

Stewart had mastered circular breathing whereby he drew air straight from his nose directly through his mouth without entering his lungs. He could hold a note for minutes.

Honey Boy doubled the rhythm.

Stewart matched.

Honey Boy quadrupled the rhythm.

Stewart matched.

Honey Boy raised the key an octave.

Stewart matched.

Honey Boy raised the key two octaves.

Stewart matched.

The two then played the "Tiger Rag" melody straight for three choruses. Each pass Honey Boy played louder. By the third pass, Stewart had given all he could, and Honey Boy's horn was easily twice as loud as Stewart's. All of the other musicians had stopped playing and the dancers had stopped dancing. They all stood around in amazement at this friendly musical duel that musicians would later refer to as "cutting contests."

The two then played the "Tiger Rag" outro, as calmly and simply as they would have at a music conservatory.

"Pretty good, for a kid," Stewart half-condescended, half-complimented Honey Boy.

Honey Boy smiled, catching his breath. "Thanks, where'd you learn to play like that?"

"Right here." Stewart pointed down at the ground.

"Why don't you play the clubs?" Honey Boy was truly curious.

Stewart rubbed his fingers together. "Money, the riverboats pay more."

"But what are the people like?"

"Society crowds, real boring—until they've had a few drinks or won some money at the card tables; then they're rowdy as anywhere."

"Can you introduce me…"

"You gotta be 18."

"I just turned 18." Honey Boy announced proudly.

"Well, I'll see what I can do, young man. I hear you're forming a marching band for Independence Day Parade. If you don't have a sax player, I'm your man. If you do, tell him to step aside, because I'm the man."

"That's right," added Red, "we should rehearse here every week."

"Well, I'll have to give up my Longshoreman's Hall gig, though."

"Let's just march it over there."

"What about the Baker girls?" asked Honey Boy.

"I'll talk to Mr. Baker," Red assured "I've known him for years."

"It's just another gig," Stewart said as he packed up his gear and retrieved his camel from the three boys who were walking it around the square. "Want a ride?"

"Where?" asked Honey Boy.

"Don't you have a gig cross town?"

"Oh, right, but I don't really know how…besides, I better hurry."

The next eleven Sundays the band gathered, except for Big Bill Black, who was on tour, so he could only make the last Sunday before the parade. The crowds grew with the reputation of the Freedom Marchers Brass Band. Little David spread various rumors about the band having made a pact with the devil or having had Julia Jackson cast a voodoo spell on the audience.

No one listened to the slander.

More and more listened to the band.

Until Independence Day came, and everyone could hear for themselves.

Red counted everyone in—*two, three, four*. The Baker girls marked time—*boom-boom-bah-boom rat-ta-tat-tat*. Professor Tony came in with a driving left hand bass line—*dih-dih-dit-dih*. Robert Stewart was the first of many to play Honey Boy's stomp riff on tenor sax—*Da-duh…da-duh…da-duh..da…duht…*

Ba-duh da duh dut dah dut dah duh duuuhh…

Doo-doo doo doo…doo doo doo dooohh…

Bwah-bwah bu-bup bup bup bup bup bup BWAAAAHHH!

Big Black Bill squeezed a chord on his accordion, then sang out a clarion call.

Forget the circumstance

No need for pomp

Come on down

To The Funky Butt Stomp

Honey Boy came in on the next verse and played so high that all the dogs, and oh there were many in Storyville, howled in unison as dulcet tones of clarity and light ascended to astral heights—higher than the 99 degree temperature that day. Honey Boy and his Freedom Marchers Brass Band more lilted than marched through his neighborhood, and on the way to the French Quarter, he caught Mother Golden's Eye and gazed longingly. He wondered off the route meandering toward her…

Everybody

Do The Funky Butt Stomp

No need to fear, Honey Boy. Your heart is open. Know your worth. You have given to your brothers and sisters. You have shared your gifts with humanity in this small planet home of ours.

You live love.

Come home.

Angel.

Romp and Roll

Roll and Romp

Now you're doin'

The Funky Butt Stomp

And dancing in Mother's arms, dreaming of Beatrice, the one who started it all did see God.

There is no devil

The angels are here

The good Lord loves you

When you do

the

Funky Butt Stomp

Please visit the author's page

http://www.lulu.com/spotlight/ericmmoberg

Made in the USA
San Bernardino, CA
05 October 2013